LISTE ..REFULLY

and Other Tales from the Therapy Room

LISTEN CAREFULLY

and Other Tales from the Therapy Room

Phil Lapworth

KARNAC

To my delightful grandson Dean

First published in 2014 by
Karnac Books Ltd
118 Finchley Road
London NW3 5HT

British Library Cataloguing in Publication Data

A C.I.P. for this book is available from the British Library

ISBN-13: 978-1-78220-217-2

Typeset by V Publishing Solutions Pvt Ltd., Chennai, India

Printed in Great Britain by TJ International Ltd, Padstow, Cornwall

www.karnacbooks.com

Contents

Contents

Introduction

This collection of ten fictional short stories invites the reader inside the consulting room, right to the heart of the therapeutic encounter, to witness what goes on between a therapist and his clients as they engage with issues such as racism, sexuality, death and dying, disfigurement, coupledom, the thrownness of life, and other existential concerns. They take us, too, inside the mind of Michael Martin, the therapist, into his internal world (including his dream world) and into the process of his supervision. Whether warm and compassionate, thoughtful and reflective, reactive and critical, or simply flying by the seat of his pants, the therapist is exposed in all his human vulnerability as he draws on his knowledge and experience in his attempts to address the concerns of his clients.

These stories intend to challenge, disturb, entertain and amuse, and to provide a rich resource for the reader's own thinking and discussion—specifically encouraged in the final chapter where the author works through each story presenting themes and theoretical aspects, and provides a series of questions for reflection. However, while psychotherapists and counsellors (whether students or qualified practitioners) will hopefully find something engaging and useful in the stories and the questions they pose, they were written also for entertainment, particularly for the entertainment of readers who are not connected with therapy in any way. Being fictional, these stories escape the confines of a textbook's clinical case examples and have free rein over the unfolding plot, yet, written by a practising psychotherapist, they have the ring of authenticity that comes from many years' experience in clinical practice. This is the second collection of short stories by Phil Lapworth. His first, *Tales From the Therapy Room—Shrink-Wrapped*, was published by Sage in 2011.

THE STORIES

Listen carefully

"And you can stuff your poxy therapy right up your fat arse!" screamed Holly, slamming the door behind her and stomping (as much as a bovver-booted stick insect could stomp) down the stairs. This seemed rather unfair. I would readily admit to a few extra pounds but my backside could hardly be described as fat. Nonetheless, I resolved again to exercise more, telling myself that this decision was entirely independent of Holly's remark. Thinking of whom, I realised I had not yet heard the front door shut. After a short silence, there came the sound of feet treading softly back upstairs. "I'm sorry," she whispered as she peered tentatively round the door. "Can I come back?"

I noticed with some relief that she had reverted to her indigenous, privately educated accent instead of what she called her "street speak", impressed as ever that she could go from County to Estuary at the drop of a hat (usually one she considered me to have dropped). "This is your session," I replied evenly. "There are about twenty minutes left." She sidled back to her seat on the sofa (the slight indentation giving only a vague indication that she'd been there before), closed her eyes and took a few deep breaths, releasing them slowly. This was one of the self-regulation techniques we'd been practising recently. I was pleased she'd thought to do it now, though it would have been more useful before her outburst. She opened her eyes and cleared her forty-a-day throat. I guess she must have got to "10" (sometimes the old ways are the best) as she started to speak. "I couldn't help it," she pleaded. "It was too much for me to hear what you said."

"You could help it," I stated matter-of-factly. "But what did you hear that you chose to run off like that?" Holly gazed at me through dark, bloodshot eyes, barely distinguishable in the surrounding blackness of her make-up. She pouted her equally black lips. I was expecting some sulky protestation about the "choice" word but, probably from her long experience of my intransigence on this score, she proved the point by changing her mind. "You said you didn't approve of my sleeping with …"

"Having sex with," I put in quickly. I hadn't said I didn't approve but I certainly didn't, and it most likely showed, so there was no point in arguing about it. Staying neutral with Holly, though always my intention, was often very difficult. Perhaps I needed to apply the "choice" theory to myself more often.

"OK, having sex with," she mimicked. "Having sex with Frank."

"Do you recall my words?" I asked.

"You're not supposed to disapprove," she asserted, avoiding my question. "You're meant to be supporting me."

"Supporting you to take care of yourself," I explained, aware that she knew full well that this was the case. "Anyway, what did I say? Do you remember?"

Holly put her finger to her forehead in a mock thinking gesture. "Something about multiple partners, something about risk. Whatever, you were judging me."

"Listen carefully. It's important. I said I was concerned that having unprotected sex with a fourth partner in the same

4

number of weeks is a very high risk. You're right. It was a judgement. It's called assessing the reality of a situation and that requires making a judgement."

"In your opinion," added Holly.

"I think you'll find it's the opinion of many people involved in sexual health," I insisted. "Apart from the risk of getting pregnant again, unprotected sex isn't safe and the more partners you have sex with the more the chance of getting an STD, including HIV."

"Like you care," remarked Holly as she chewed a strand of hair that had fallen from the dark, hair-gripped mound piled high on her head like candyfloss. I thought how attractive she could look if only she would look after herself, if only she would care.

"You think I don't care?" I asked.

"I guess you do," she answered. "You couldn't put up with me if you didn't."

Holly, now twenty-five, had discovered when she was thirteen that, apart from potentially being pleasurable, sex made her feel wanted, at least momentarily. Unfortunately, being wanted lasted only as long as she was willing to have sex and she had never experienced an ongoing relationship with anyone, including her much older stepbrother, who was the first to have sex with her. The pattern was deeply entrenched: meet a man, have instantaneous sex, feel wanted, have more sex, feel more wanted, then (usually the next morning) want to be wanted for more than sex, feel used and aggrieved when this appears not to be the case, become angry and vitriolic, and end up demonising each man who had started out as the most wonderful man in the world.

"Frank's different," she claimed.

I raised my eyebrows. "Oh yes? How different?"

"I don't know," she replied. "Just different."

"Come on Holly," I exhorted. "They're always different."

"No, really," she insisted, "Frank's very different. His parents are friends of my parents. He's no stranger. I've known him all my life."

This was indeed different. Holly's tendency was to pick up total strangers in rough bars on the seedier side of Bristol: a habit we'd explored many times and speculatively discerned that the appeal lay in its danger (usually drunk, she felt a "rush" from the risk of approach), the denigration she felt afterwards (repeating her early abuse), and a rebellious pleasure in doing something of which her parents (and I) would strongly disapprove. So maybe this was different. Maybe Holly was growing up and calming down. A childhood friend as her lover might provide the continuity and consistency that so far had been sadly lacking.

"And we had breakfast together before he left his flat this morning," she added, as if this was the proof I needed in order to be convinced. Sceptically, I could think of a number of reasons he might have breakfasted, hunger being number one (and satisfying one's appetite did not constitute romantic commitment as far as I was concerned).

"And how old is Frank?" I asked, aware that I'd assumed them to be of similar age.

"Why?" Holly responded.

"I'm curious to learn just how different he is from the others," I said.

"Age isn't important," she pouted. "He thinks I'm very mature."

"So he's another middle-aged man?" I asked, already knowing the answer.

"Fifty is the new forty," she replied.

"And is twenty-five the new fifteen?"

"Fuck off!" she said in instant Estuary and then reverted to County to add. "Good heavens, you're so passé."

"So he's twice your age."

Holly raised her black eyes to the ceiling as if calculating hard. "Well, let me see, two times twenty-five, now, um, um, yes, I think that makes fifty." I ignored her sarcasm and pressed on. "And how old was your brother when he first abused you at thirteen?"

"I see where you're heading, Mr. Einstein," she pouted. "But it doesn't work like that. He was twenty-six at the time. Yes, twice my age then—but now he's only thirty-eight, so not that much older than me. As I said, age is irrelevant. Anyway, you're probably three times older than me, and I'm still here after two years, aren't I?"

Sometimes it was hard to resist responding to Holly's provocations. There was no problem with her mathematical ability, only her deliberate miscalculation and aggravating intention. I reminded myself that I had a choice and took a few slow, deep breaths, practising the same self-regulation technique she'd used earlier. I knew she wanted me to rise to the bait and get into an almighty slanging match like the ones she had with her parents and her transient lovers, but I knew she also needed me to remain calm and non-attacking if we were to make further inroads into her own tendency towards impulsivity rather than thought.

"Yes, that's true," I said. "It's a different sort of relationship we've evolved and you've shown real commitment to it. I'm just not sure that Frank will make a commitment to you."

Holly did not respond but for the remaining ten minutes sat and stared out of the window. Her time up, she rose and left without a word. Unusually, she did not try to wheedle out more time by bringing up something in the last minute, nor did she slam the doors behind her: both potential signs that she was at least reflecting on our exchange rather than just reacting to it.

It was the times she stormed out angrily and noisily that worried me more as these were the times I'd either get a call from A & E informing me she'd overdosed or she'd return to the next session with scars along the inside of her arms. I had never remarked upon either, which may sound strange but, from the start, I'd experienced these gestures not so much as serious threats to her life (at no time had she needed her stomach pumping, nor were her scars deep enough to be life-threatening) but, apart from giving her release and relief, more as a means of inducing me to be either angry or over-solicitously caring or even remorseful for what I might have challenged her with in the previous session. The strategy seemed to be working, though a hard one for me to maintain in the face of such a "cry for help". Many months had passed since she'd last overdosed or cut herself. The fact that today she'd managed to weather her internal storm and return to the session was an indication of progress.

Holly's background, even before the abuse, was complex and inconsistent. Her father had disappeared when her emotionally demanding mother had become pregnant, leaving her to cope alone with her baby and her feelings. I surmised that Holly became the object of her mother's self-serving love and hate from the start. Though Holly's childhood memories—of cuddling her mother to soothe her distress and being pushed away when Holly herself had needs—begin much later, her prolific nightmares in which a neonate mouse, cat, dog or human is almost smothered to death by an inept carer, then abandoned to fend for herself (often in cold climates), suggested the even earlier extremes of her mother's unpredictable and selfish parenting.

When Holly was four-years-old, her mother met and quickly married an affluent older man and moved into his family mansion where his three much older sons still lived. Now Holly really was left in a cold climate. Her mother no longer needed her comfort and support; the poor nurture that Holly had experienced was suddenly withdrawn and she was left to her own devices, a stranger in a loveless environment where only the sexual attentions of one of her stepbrothers provided any semblance of warmth. Ironically, being sent away to boarding school at the age of seven could have given her the opportunity to feel a sense of safety and belonging, but this turned out to be an equally cold environment in which sexual abuse by the male staff—from tutors to gardeners—was shockingly endemic. For vulnerable Holly, it was a case of plus ça change ...

Frank's dalliance with Holly was over by the time we next met. His sadistic sexual demands had become too great for her. Perhaps it was a sign her self-esteem was increasing, however minutely, that she had put a stop to the abuse much sooner than with the previous men in her life.

"What a tosser!" she exclaimed.

"The same Frank who was so different and mature?" I asked, wanting her to see the extremes of her perceptions.

"Yeah, yeah, rub it in," she said with a defeated sigh.

"I'm sorry, I don't mean to," I replied. "At least, not in the way you mean. I guess I do want to 'rub in' your experience so that it's there for you to refer to as a warning. As it is, you somehow don't let it in, so each time it feels like it's different."

"I'm starting to see it," she said softly. "I can see the pattern right now. I know I keep repeating it. But at the time ... I don't know."

"What goes on in that moment?" I asked. "Where does your knowledge of the pattern go?"

"Oh, it's out the window. That part of me just isn't there. It's gone totally."

"Who is there?" I asked.

"Me? It feels like me. It feels like it's the real me. I come alive. Someone wants me. Someone seems to care and I throw myself at them like they're a life raft. They'll save me from drowning. They must save me. I don't want to drown."

"And yet ..." I began.

"Fuck, fuck, fuck, fuck, fuck!" exclaimed Holly.

"I wonder ..."

"Blah, blah, blah, blah, blah! I know what you're going to say. You've said it all before and I know exactly what I need to do. But ..."

"But?"

"But I'm a wreck. I need a fucking life raft because I'm a fucking wreck!" she sobbed.

"You're not a wreck," I contradicted vehemently. "Holly, you are not a wreck. I know you feel like a wreck at times but that's because you sail into storms of your own making. You wreck yourself."

I hadn't meant to say this. I certainly thought it was true but I hadn't intended to let the thought be said aloud. It felt harsh and I wasn't sure that it had any therapeutic value. On the one hand, I was stating the obvious; on the other, the obvious is sometimes too cruel. Timing is everything and I was sure I'd mistimed this accusation. It was a bit like saying "you weren't looking where you were going" to someone lying bleeding under the wheels of a car—true but unhelpful. I was thinking of a way of softening those last three words, but Holly, who so often did not listen very carefully (and may not have heard my words at all), spoke first.

"Like a child," she said. Her eyes looked towards the window but were not seeing outside, more focusing on something inside her own head.

I encouraged her to say more.

"Like a toddler," she said as she moved her gaze towards me. "I've seen a toddler get told off, I don't know, like for accidentally spilling something. The mother shouts, 'Be more careful you stupid girl!'—and the little girl trips and hurts herself badly."

"Have I said the equivalent of the mother's words?" I asked, still unsure if she'd heard them or not.

Holly looked puzzled. "Oh I see, no, 'you wreck yourself' is what the girl does, it describes the girl's actions. You were right. It's what I do."

"I see," I said, hoping I did. "So the girl deliberately hurts herself in response to the telling off. What's the girl trying to say to her mother when she hurts herself?"

"She's saying, 'I know you hate me because I'm bad but maybe you'll love me if I'm hurting.'"

"Maybe you'll love me if I'm hurting," I repeated, and saw that Holly's black eyes were awash with tears.

This seemed like a pivotal session for Holly. She had unearthed a vital understanding of herself, an explanation that gave meaning to her behaviour not just as reckless self-wrecking but as a plea for her mother's love. It was not the searching for love with men that was the prime motivation (I suspect on some level she knew from the start it was not going to work out with these unsuitable lovers). It was the inevitable wrecking that would follow. And at the core of all this was her belief that if she suffered enough in these violent encounters her mother would love her—although she never really had and probably never would. Like the mother in Holly's story, her own mother simply shouted at her, often abusively, and Holly would then "trip and hurt herself badly", and more so. She would escalate to cutting and overdosing, wrecking herself more in her doomed attempts to be cared for.

For some time we sailed on calmer waters. Outside the therapy (in "the real world" as she liked to put it), Holly stopped frequenting bars in her self-wrecking search to feel wanted. Instead, she reconnected with a few old school friends and joined in their less harmful pastimes that seemed to mostly consist of listening to illegally downloaded music and spending hours chatting on the Internet trying to decide what they might do if they weren't chatting on the Internet. I could see this wasn't going to satisfy Holly for long. Less harmful meant less risky and so, in order to pre-empt Holly's need for excitement and incident, I suggested she might find some activity that would satisfy such need.

"What do you suggest?" she asked immediately, as if the idea appealed to her.

"Well, what do you think would be good?" I asked in reply, hoping she wasn't really expecting me to come up with something, not just because it wouldn't be therapeutic for me to do her thinking for her but also because an annual visit to the seaside was about the limit of my need for excitement and incident. This, I suspected, was a far cry from Holly's—and I was right.

"Hang-gliding!" she suggested enthusiastically. "I've always liked the idea of hang-gliding. Don't you think that would be great?"

"Indeed it would!" I replied, trying to match her enthusiasm and stifling the question "But is it safe?" that I so wanted to ask her. It would have missed the point entirely. And yet, I was aware of the pattern that she'd recently recognised and I was concerned that perhaps my keenness for her to find some excitement in her life might also have provided her with the perfect excuse to wreck herself—even to kill herself.

It seems I needn't have worried. Holly took to hang-gliding as if she'd been born with wings. I admired how diligently she researched what schools were available, joined a club in Bristol, and went through an intensive course of training. After some months of instruction she made her first flight over what I now know is called the Bath Gap. Numerous flights ensued and it was apparent that Holly was hooked. She spent many of our sessions recounting her adventures in various parts of the country where she was meeting and making friends with people of her own age who matched her enthusiasm for the sport much more than I could. I began to wonder if I was becoming redundant as Holly engaged in the outside world like never before.

There were several other signs that Holly was changing. On a physical level she looked much fitter and healthier, having stopped smoking, joined a gym (hang-gliding requiring muscular strength), and gained some much needed weight (nothing extreme, but the stick insect was transforming into something more akin to a grasshopper). She looked different in other ways, like letting her hair free from its previous architectural structure to fall around her unmade-up face. Amazingly too, her bovver boots were replaced by trainers, and her jeans were sometimes blue rather than black. Even her T-shirts reflected celebration rather than mourning in her choice of colours and slogans, though I was not too sure about "Bring Back Hanging", even though the logo beneath was of a hang-glider. I preferred the more positive double entendre of "Hang Loose".

On an emotional level, Holly was increasingly more stable, and when not was less extreme. Her excited pleasure was palpable but not overly dramatic, and her anger was passionate but not full of rage. There were times when her stability was tested—especially by weeks of bad weather when gliding was impossible, or by her mother's continuing dismissive and toxic remarks. But she would use her therapy sessions constructively to work through any feelings with which she was struggling, finding beneath them her grief at what she had had to endure in her childhood, and letting her sadness be expressed. She even tolerated my two-week Easter break, feeling sad but not devastated, and returned willing to explore and talk about her feelings rather than damn poxy therapy (and me) to hell as she had many times before.

In light of all these encouraging developments, my concern for Holly in her choice of such an extreme sport gradually faded. She seemed well aware of the risks and took care to follow all the safety procedures and vigilantly select the best flying areas and times. I detected nothing reckless in her approach to hang-gliding to give me cause to worry. Though, of course, accidents happen.

And that was how I described to myself my fall from a ladder when the weight of the wisteria flowers in May had pulled away the trellis from the wall and I had sought to fix it. I don't think I was reckless. I'd put bricks against the bottom legs of the ladder to stop it slipping. I'd angled the ladder according to the manual that had come with it. I wore rubber-soled shoes that had a good grip. What I failed to check was the clasp that secures the extension to the base part of the ladder. All I remember was a sudden veering to the left, madly grasping at the wisteria to prevent my fall, and then the sight of the concrete path coming up to meet me. Nothing more.

I was in hospital for a week and discharged with the caution not to return to work for at least a further two weeks (which I might well have done had it not been forbidden by my family). I felt mentally fit enough, but I had been concussed—referred to by the medics as Mild Traumatic Brain Injury, which sounded much worse—and this was of more concern to them and my family than the broken ribs and severe cuts and bruises to my limbs, which I found the more painful. Under much protestation, I acquiesced.

Fortunately, I did not have to inform my clients myself of the interruption to our work. I think I would have found talking to all of them rather a strain. On gaining consciousness, I was grateful to learn that my colleague and professional executor had immediately phoned my clients and informed them simply that I would be indisposed for at least three weeks and to phone nearer the time to check if I would be available.

Several had accepted this news with disappointment and understanding, others with great concern and a frustrated desire to know more details, and yet others with an irritated suspicion that I might be skiving (which, in fact, once out of hospital, I considered I was—so I felt some empathy for their viewpoint). The responses were multitudinous and individual and said a great deal about my clients' unique personalities and their ways of seeing the world. In particular, their reactions to my absence gave some deeper insight into their relationships with others, especially their parents and partners.

I was curious to learn of Holly's reaction but she had not answered her mobile, and my colleague, after several attempts, had simply left a message without going into details.

Holly did not make any contact during my convalescence. Knowing she had probably not listened carefully to the message my colleague had left, I left my own message to confirm I would be returning to work the following week but she did not turn up. I waited for fifteen minutes for her to arrive and then phoned as is my practice. Having allowed myself all manner of catastrophic fantasies, I was relieved when she answered.

"Holly, this is Michael."

"Yeah? What is it?" she said, as if I was intruding on something far more important.

"I was expecting to see you today for our session."

"Oh, was it today?" she queried nonchalantly. "You're back then?"

"Yes, I started back this week," I replied, already detecting from her "street" tone that she was not in a good place. "Did you not get my message?"

"Might have," she muttered. "Can't remember."

"I could see you later today," I offered, aware I was overstepping the consistent boundary I'd so carefully drawn throughout our work but feeling concerned that my unplanned absence had triggered her relapse.

"Busy today," she said abruptly, and then added to what I was already feeling as a slap in the face, "I might come next week. I'll see."

"I look forward to seeing you then," I said, though this was only half true, the other truth was that I was not looking forward to seeing her at all, not even wanting to see her. To my shame, in my hurt and anger at Holly's response, I felt her mother's selfish love and toxic hate rise in me with the force of a tsunami. I put down the phone without saying more.

Two things emerged from my supervision later that week when I talked of this exchange between Holly and myself. The first was the similarity between Holly's mother and my own. They shared a common parenting style where the offspring are used as alternating carers and combatants in a bid to meet their own unmet needs of childhood. Recognising my own experience at the hands of such a mother, and the concomitant "presence" of such a mother within me that could be drawn upon in retaliation—within myself, or with another—helped me disentangle what was mine and what was Holly's. The second was the realisation that this dynamic was also within Holly. Her retaliation for being abandoned by me, however temporarily, was to treat me as her mother had treated her. She was letting me know what it feels like to be left in a cold climate.

Though my supervision had assisted me greatly in reaching a calmer and more stable place within myself, I was still somewhat anxious before Holly's arrival. I reminded myself of the "rule of thumb"—"it's never as bad as it seems and it's never as good as it seems"—that I'd found useful in the past when working with Holly and others who have suffered the yo-yoing engulfment and abandonment of a mother who sees her offspring as a lover and a rival, a source of comfort and of threat. I held on to the first part of this rule while acknowledging I had probably not paid enough heed to the precariousness of what had recently seemed so good for Holly. I had counted my chickens too soon and it seemed they had come home to roost.

Holly had not reverted completely to her gothic style (though she was wearing her bovver boots) but she was unkempt when, much to my relief, she arrived for her session. Her hair looked lank and unwashed and her clothes uncared for. She wore no make-up but her face looked tired and drawn as if she hadn't slept in days. However, she did not appear anywhere near as wrecked as I'd imagined her when we spoke on the phone and I was reassured to notice that her arms gave no indication that she'd been cutting.

Less anxious at seeing her, I felt I was speaking honestly when I said, "It's good to see you back."

Holly did not respond. She gazed at the floor in a kind of stupor. I waited but I knew she could out-silence me until the end of the session as she had done in the early days.

"You seem angry with me," I suggested after a while. "I guess my sudden absence was difficult for you."

"No," she shouted, suddenly sitting upright and looking me in the eye. "I'm not angry, I'm fucking furious!"

"OK, tell me about it. Tell me about your fury," I said. Then, not wanting to encourage her escalation and, perhaps even more, not wanting to be on the receiving end of her full-force rage, added, "But you can tell me without shouting. My hearing is fine and I very much want to hear you so please don't deafen me."

I was not sure how Holly might take these last comments and was thankful when I noticed a fleeting smile cross her face. "I'm furious," she exclaimed in her County voice and in a quieter tone, the smile long gone and her mouth now downturned. "I'm furious because you think it's perfectly fine to take a break and cancel sessions on a whim—and for three weeks! And to get someone else to do your dirty work for you! You couldn't even be bothered to phone me yourself so what does that say about our committed relationship?"

Her voice had become slightly louder with each word but she still kept control of herself and did not escalate to screaming as she might have done in the past. Even so, I felt like a naughty child being scolded by a mother and I could hear and feel my aggrieved defences rising in a retaliatory onslaught in which I wanted to shout her down. But I had invited her to express her fury and I was cognisant of the fact that there was a significant advance in her being here directly expressing her feelings to me rather than more dramatically displaying them through cutting or wrecking herself with drugs. Paradoxically, I considered her anger was a sign that she felt cared for enough,

17

generally, in order to express how she had not felt cared for, specifically, by my absence. Tempted though I was, I did not defend myself by correcting her assumptions. Her experience was more important than whatever had happened to me.

"You thought I'd not cared enough to talk to you myself," I paraphrased. "That must have seemed hurtful and I'm sorry you felt that way."

"Like fuck!" said Holly with only half the venom such an expletive usually held.

"No, I mean it," I said gently. "It must have been awful for you to feel so uncared for, like you were thoughtlessly left out in the cold."

"It was," she replied. "You were doing to me what my mother always did—not giving a fuck how I felt, just looking after yourself without a thought for me."

"You felt I didn't hold you in mind," I reflected.

"I felt you'd abandoned me," she said almost inaudibly as her anger turned to tears. "I felt so abandoned I wanted to cut myself again."

"I can see that you didn't," I said, wanting her to know I'd noticed.

"No, I didn't," she said almost proudly. "My hurting never worked with my mother. It didn't make her love me."

"And with me?" I asked.

"No, it never worked with you either," she replied, wiping her eyes, her face looking clearer and refreshed. "You're a bastard! You just ignore my wounds!"

"Do I?" There was a pause.

"Well, the physical ones," she said eventually, managing a faint smile. "I guess with you I don't need to get attention that way."

"But you didn't feel like that while I was away," I reminded her, in case she'd moved too quickly away from her anger with me.

"No, it was hard to hold on to any belief that you cared a damn about me," she said, sounding more sad than angry. "I tried to. I talked to myself and I told myself not to take it personally, that you were away from your other clients too, that I could survive three weeks without therapy ..."

"But ...?" I asked.

"But to take a fucking holiday at the drop of a hat!" she shouted. "What's that all about? Surely it's unethical to do that, just to go off without warning! How can you justify doing that to me?"

On hearing the word "holiday" I decided that not to correct her assumption at this point, though useful so far in allowing her to express her feelings, was tantamount to lying. Exploring fantasies is often essential in uncovering unconscious processes, but withholding the reality of the situation now began to feel like an unnecessary and unkind manipulation. "I can't justify it at all," I said, "If I'd taken a holiday without notice, I would be unable to find any justification."

"What do you mean '*if*'?" she challenged. "That woman's message said you were on holiday."

I was perplexed, and said so, "I don't understand what my colleague could have said to give that impression ..."

"No, it wasn't just an impression," insisted Holly. "She clearly said you were away somewhere for three weeks."

"I'm baffled ..."

"Somewhere, I don't know ... it began with 'D'," she went on. "She said you would be in this place for three weeks. She gave the impression it could be even longer. I wonder why ... was it if the weather stayed hot in this exotic resort?"

During this flight of fancy, the penny had suddenly dropped for me. I found it hard not to smile—but I didn't want to shame her. I thought of other times when, almost willfully, she had not listened carefully, where a dismissive "whatever!" in street speak had been all she'd needed to deflect from her mistake.

19

Given what she'd been through this time, I wasn't so sure she'd be able to brush this one away so lightly.

"Holly," I said as gently as I could. "I think you may have misheard what my colleague said. You see, she told me she'd said exactly the same to all my clients. What she said was that I would be *indisposed for three weeks.*"

"There you are," said Holly defiantly. "In … In … In … where? No! No! No! She didn't say that! She's lying!"

"I'm sure that's what she said," I replied softly.

Holly sat totally still and silent. I was worried that she was feeling humiliated and that her freeze reaction was her attempt at protecting herself. But suddenly she moved and exclaimed, "The only place I can think of right now that sounds remotely like 'disposed' is Desborough—really exotic, huh? What the fuck would you be doing holidaying in a Midlands backwater like Desborough?" She said all this in a harsh self-deprecating way and fell silent again.

For some moments I was concerned that her former anger towards me had turned upon herself. I noticed her shoulders trembling slightly—was she going to let herself cry or was her shaking a sign of fury, even fear? Gradually, her trembling increased to shaking and soon her whole body was convulsing and her hands flew to her mouth as if to stop herself retching. Alarmed, I was about to intervene with the wastebasket for her to vomit into when, quite unexpectedly, I realised she was laughing. Perhaps it was because my anxiety needed to be released too or perhaps it was the infectious nature of *her* laughter but, either way, I started laughing too. I wasn't quite sure why Desborough was so funny but I wasn't particularly bothered. It just was. And every time we calmed down and were about to speak, one of us would burst out convulsively laughing again, tears rolling down our cheeks. We simply could not stop. It lasted for at least ten minutes until the session was up and Holly left still giggling.

I'm aware of the stress-reducing benefits of laughter therapy and I believe that humour, used appropriately and sensitively, has a rightful and important place in the consulting room—but what occurred in those few minutes between Holly and myself could not have been orchestrated or foreseen. They turned out to be more valuable than many months of therapy.

The effects were indelibly felt and tangibly influential in our ensuing work together. It was not simply stress-reducing for each of us to have laughed in that moment, nor was it just an enjoyable passing pleasure. I think it was the reciprocal experience—the intimacy, the spontaneity, the allowing of our defences to drop—that catapulted our work together to a new level of openness and trust from then on. It seems to me that listening carefully may often be sensible and wise, but sometimes being care-less, as we were that day, can have amazing repercussions.

Uncoupled

A crucial quality required of a therapist working with couples is that of neutrality—unfortunately, I just don't have it. I worked with couples for many years but I was always aware of struggling hard not to favour one member of the couple over the other. In time, it proved impossible (and, I had to admit, unethical) for me to continue even to try. It reached a point where no sooner had a couple entered my consulting room than I would find myself taking sides. With straight couples my allegiance was more often than not with the female rather than the male partner. Faced with an emotionally literate and reflective woman alongside an emotionally stunted man who if he could string more than two words together at all would rather be talking about the stock market or the Championship League Table, it seemed obvious to me to say to the woman, "This guy is a waste of space! Get the hell out now!" I didn't actually say this of course but I undoubtedly thought it, and this is not the sort of attitude they teach you on the Relate course.

Of course, there must have been some reason for these women to choose the men they had. In some instances it had been an obvious matter of stunning good looks, in others of substantial wealth, and in some, having reached an age where childbearing was a race against the biological clock, it was a case of finding an available, hopefully fertile, partner. I could see the rationale but at the same time I questioned whether it was worth the price of living within such an otherwise unfulfilling, unloving, sometimes tempestuous but, more often than not, tedious relationship.

But this wasn't just a sex thing. Equally with male or female gay couples, I found I favoured one partner over the other: invariably the one who expressed their feelings—the emotionally articulate one who could describe their experiences from their heart. This was the key to my discrimination. Whether straight or gay, I was drawn to the partner who could feel and make their feelings known rather than the logical, computerised partner who lived life in their head. While I could work well enough with the "heady" ones in individual therapy, put them in the same room with a partner (with whom I could compare and contrast) and I was incapable of neutrality. Working with couples became untenable for me and I stopped offering this service (or disservice as it became) some years ago.

And yet, naturally enough, along with other troubled aspects of their lives, individuals bring relationship issues to therapy. They want to explore the problems they're having with their partners: sometimes to find ways of improving the situation, sometimes just to air their complaints in an "*Ain't it awful?*" kind of way. Such psychological pastimes or games are ubiquitous within most couples' patterns of relating. There's the "*I always … she or he never …*" variety, often to do with the division of domestic labour or the initiation of sex. Or the "*I should have listened to (insert name of relative or friend here)*" where supposedly the third party had warned all along of the partner's shortcomings. But this two-to-one majority view lasts only for a moment as the defending partner drags up the support of *their* numerous relatives and friends to provide the counterweight retaliation, and so on.

Then there's the even more prevalent "*If it weren't for you ...*" type of game where all manner of astounding accomplishments would have been achieved were it not for the disabling shortcomings of the partner. I once had a female client blame her feckless husband for thwarting her ambition of becoming prima ballerina with the Royal Ballet. Try as I might, I couldn't quite see how this useless man had managed to prevent this achievement, especially given other more likely mitigating factors (which my client conveniently chose to ignore)—above all, her short stature and rotund girth.

I used to address these common dynamics of coupledom quite well with individual clients. It was often a case of exploring what these games were really trying to achieve beyond the surface-level competition for supremacy. What unacknowledged part of themselves did they see in their partners and need to learn about? What was it that my clients wanted in relation to their partners that they were not overtly asking for? What did they think their partners wanted from them that was not being openly addressed?

More often than not, the answer to these last two questions was summed up in a single word—"love". But while it may be a breakthrough to admit to a lack of love, it's too general a word to be of much use in the nitty-gritty practicalities of relationships.

What our work would hopefully evolve into was a more detailed exploration of what was missing in their relationship that left them feeling unloved, and of how they might now experience being loved. For some, this was simply a warm smile in greeting or a hug at the end of the day. For others, some acknowledgement of their professional or child-caring role, or both. For yet others, it involved the total reconstruction of a relationship that had become stale with familiarity.

"Love" and its expression would often mean very different things to each partner and needed sensitive negotiation. For many clients this exploration of the present would lead to the deficiencies in their childhood experiences, and, once there, we were on a roll.

Addressing these early needs in therapy—the need of attention, recognition, understanding, acceptance (all easily subsumed under the word "love")—liberated them to address their current needs in their adult relationships. Maturity is hard to achieve if one partner (or both, as is often the case) demands that their unmet needs of childhood be totally fulfilled by the other. The relationship becomes like a nursery playground without adult supervision: primitive, noisy, and very messy.

In this expansion from childhood deficits to adult maturity, I enjoy the challenge of working with an individual on their own development and, vicariously, on that of their relationship. Without the presence of the partner, I can be much more balanced in my view of them; more able to emphasise the joint creation of problems and the need for joint solutions, particularly the very simple yet so difficult one of truly listening to each other. I might go so far as to say that I am a competent couple therapist when working with individuals.

However, there is one notable exception. For the sake of anonymity I shall call him Victor, not because of any sense of him as a conqueror, more that I'd invented a new diagnostic classification for him, namely Meldroid personality disorder (after the notoriously grumpy character in *One Foot in the Grave*).

One might argue that the category of major depression already covers this disorder, as there seem to be several overlapping features—depressed mood, diminished pleasure, fatigue, etc.—but the key to my differential diagnosis (and my new classification) is the concomitant existence of the opposite of all these qualities. In other words, there is enjoyment, pleasure and energy in relation to the very lack of them.

In my experience, depressed people talk in a depressed way about their lives but they do not have the energy to complain. Conversely, my client Victor not only had the energy for complaint, he positively (or perhaps I should say, negatively) thrived on it. I suppose the term "sadomasochistic personality" could have described my client to some degree but I preferred my "Meldroid personality" as it avoided drifting into physical or sexual realms (which my client altogether lacked) and sounded much kinder and less pathological.

But my preference was mostly due to the fact that he was so much the epitome of the lugubrious Victor Meldrew. I found it hard to think of him any other way. The majority of his complaints converged around his wife (I shall call her Margaret to continue the TV sitcom analogy), and his complaints of her, most of all, seemed to afford him a martyrish pleasure, an excited vitality that coexisted alongside his depressed mood.

Though still in his early fifties, Victor looked and sounded like a world weary octogenarian as he arrived in my consulting room for the first time. His skin had a sallow, unhealthy complexion and his body, beneath a shabby suit at least two sizes too big, seemed shrunken and lost within it. His heavy, black-rimmed spectacles were far too big for his tiny, hollow-cheeked face, magnifying his eyes so much that he reminded me of a bush baby—though sadly lacking any cuteness that might have induced some endearment to him on my part.

To be truthful, I felt rather repulsed by him as in a high, reedy monotone he reeled off his catalogue of complaints. I think it was during this outpouring that I came up with my new diagnostic category. I'd noticed that as the list of complaints grew, Victor's delivery changed. If I were to annotate a piece of music with directions to describe the change, I'd somehow indicate a gradual progression from *freddo* to *con brio*—the latter coming into full force when the topic under consideration moved from his work environment via bodily ailments to life at home with his wife.

"She sent me here," he said in conclusion to his several complaints of her—which ranged from slovenliness, untidiness and poor mathematical ability (he was an accountant) to over-emotionality and bad taste in literature (which turned out

27

to be her love of novels in contrast to his liking for political biographies) and many others in between. Apparently spent of his diatribe, he reverted to his slumped posture that, a few moments previously, could almost have been described as alert.

"Your wife sent you?" I queried.

"She did. She said if I don't change, I'll be the death of her," he replied without expression.

"That sounds like she's rather desperate for you to change," I commented. "But, apart from Margaret's insistence, is there anything else that brings you here? I mean, is there anything you'd like to change for you?"

"No, not really," came his dismal reply. "I don't see much point."

"Apart from keeping your wife alive?" I checked.

"Not even that," he sighed. "It might be a relief if she wasn't."

Did I notice a slight grin on Victor's tiny pinched face following that remark? Or was it more of a wince? I'm not sure. But I was sure there was no point in working with some-one who'd been sent by his wife, found fault in everyone but himself and had no motivation to change at all, and I said as much. I noticed my relief at the thought of not working with him.

"So you see me as a hopeless case," he moaned, "I think my wife does too."

"No, I don't think that at all," I replied instantly though not entirely honestly, having already sided with his wife in my mind. "The problem is that you haven't presented yourself as a 'case' to be hopeless about. It seems the world is at fault rather than you. The 'case' seems to be other people and they're not here in therapy. While you don't have a case, there's nothing to work with. Unless, of course, you're here because you really do want to explore something, perhaps to change something for yourself, and not just for Margaret."

"I do," he admitted. "I want to be more confident."

I didn't fully believe him. It was too fast a turn around. I suspected he'd grasped at something, anything, simply to satisfy my need for him to have a plausible problem to work with in order to be in therapy. In this way, he could placate his distressed wife and maintain a forum in which he could legitimately contact his vitality in negative self-expression. But at least he'd introduced something to do with himself and not just complaints about others. Perhaps there was some hope in that, I thought.

But what a foolish hope that turned out to be. In the following weeks, I learnt more about the shortcomings of his poor, long-suffering wife (for that's definitely how I saw her) than gained any insight into Victor's espoused desire to become more confident. It seemed to me, at least in relation to complaining, he was overly confident. If only we could turn the spotlight on his own shortcomings (of which I had already compiled quite a catalogue) rather than everyone else's, especially his wife's, we might find some understanding of his need for complaint. I was well aware by now that if Margaret had been here with him in couple therapy, I'd definitely be thinking, if not saying, "This guy is a waste of space! Get the hell out now!" For she was clearly the emotionally literate one, the one who spoke from her heart—unlike Victor who spoke from his head, and a very small head at that.

As the weeks went on, I became aware that Victor's complaints against Margaret were escalating to a pitch that began increasingly to concern me. My anxiety was for Margaret rather than Victor as I began to consider that his constant negativity might well drive her to her death: by some slow, lingering, life-draining malaise, if not by suicide. It seemed to me, in his estimation, she could not do a thing right. If she tried to discuss politics, she was too ill-informed. If she cooked a new recipe, she didn't understand the subtleties of French cuisine. And when she bought tickets for a performance of Delius' *Requiem*, she should have known he considered Delius a third-rate composer whose music was far too watery and romantic. His high-pitched voice meowed like a circling buzzard—but more complaintive than plaintive, more resentful than sad—as he protested her incompetence.

"I wonder if there's any sense in which you could see Margaret's gestures, however off target, as loving and caring?" I enquired tentatively. "Might her intention be to please you rather than get things wrong for you?"

Victor hardly paused for thought. "It's deliberate," he stated firmly. "She does it on purpose."

"She purposely does things knowing you'll be disturbed by them?" I asked, attempting to stay neutral but knowing my tone betrayed that I thought the idea improbable. "Do you have any idea why she would do this?"

Victor hesitated. He picked a speck of fluff from his ill-fitting jacket before answering. His answer took me by surprise.

"Because she's sadomasochistic," he said categorically.

Having sat for weeks on end listening to what could easily be described as his sadistic attacks upon Margaret (though simultaneously sounding like the masochistic victim in his delivery), I struggled to get to grips with what appeared to me to be a topsy-turvy perception. I'd heard nothing to suggest that Margaret might be the persecutory type, in fact, just the opposite. In my mind she remained the long-suffering, frail and innocent victim trapped in a life-sapping relationship.

Though I'd tried several times previously, and unsuccessfully, to uncover some historical dimension to Victor's way of being, especially in relation to his view of himself as lacking confidence, I thought it was time to make another attempt in response to this latest revelation. "I know so little about your mother," I said. "But I wonder if you experienced her as sado-masochistic?" This instantly touched a nerve. The tirade that followed contained expletives of which I'd not thought Victor capable. Complaining he may be, but not given to the profanity and vulgarity of the obscene vocabulary that now emanated from his spittle-flecked lips.

His description of his mother's wicked and violent behaviour towards him, and her relentless portrayal of herself nonetheless as the suffering victim, beggared belief—but believe him I did. In that instant, the revulsion I'd felt towards him for so long vanished. The shrunken man with the bush baby eyes that now held some endearment as he sat exhausted from his outburst, wept silently. I too felt sad and ashamed at my lack, until this moment, of empathy. I should have remained faithful to the knowledge that no one avoids developing a personality, however likeable or unattractive that personality may be, without the inevitable influence of childhood.

Victor may have been a difficult person to warm to and work with, but had I been less judgemental in my response to him I could have seen much earlier the battered child beneath his defences. Thankfully, it was not too late. Now he was showing his emotional life openly we could start the real work of therapy—the expression and release of a lifetime's anger and distress.

It was not easy going though; not a case of instant transformational release through catharsis as is often presented in the movies. However, bit by bit, forwards and backwards, round and round, Victor became more like the clients I mentioned earlier—the emotionally articulate ones who address their experience from the heart. He had a lot of emotion to express and, though always tempted by his logical mind to go off into cognitive excursions, he was sporadically able to cry and rage and grieve for the child who deserved so much better than the treatment he'd received at the hands (and I should add, tongue and stick) of his selfish and sadistic yet martyrish mother who went unchecked by his passive, ineffectually complaining and downtrodden father.

Victor's head came into its own when looking at patterns. He discerned without my prompting that in his relationship with Margaret he was possibly projecting many of his mother's behaviours onto her while simultaneously modelling himself on his father. In such manner, he was repeating his parents' pattern of relationship as well as reliving his childhood relationship with his mother. Updating his perceptions, he could see that maybe Margaret was not deliberately doing things to annoy him and that she may simply be trying to get it right for him. He began to see her in a more benign light, to accept her good intentions even if sometimes, as with Delius, they were way off the mark.

By the end of our first year working together, Victor and Margaret's relationship had reportedly much improved. They were doing things together—going out dancing, going to social events in the neighbourhood, meeting and befriending other people (for Victor's sour view of others was sweetening too).

"I'm feeling so much more confident," said a smiling, younger-looking Victor recently. "I can see the world as much less threatening and I'm finding I have a place in it."

"That's wonderful," I remarked enthusiastically. "It seems obvious now that your lack of confidence was linked to your mother's threatening behaviour. It's understandable that you saw the whole world as hostile in response to her treatment of you. How could you feel confident in such a world?"

"No, it was quite impossible," agreed Victor. "But I disguised my fear of it through complaining about it, didn't I?"

"I think you did," I concurred, admiring his insight. "I think we often hide our fear by being critical and judgemental."

"Like you were of me when I first came here," stated Victor starkly.

I felt my stomach turn as he said these words. Now *he* had hit a nerve. I felt the shame I'd felt previously on hearing Victor's emotional revelations about his cruel mother. My immediate, defensive reaction was to think how to deny his accurate portrayal—but I knew such a disingenuous response was not what Victor deserved.

"Yes," I confessed. "You're right about that. I'm sorry. I feel mortified that I judged you so dismissively. It must have been disappointing for you to have me respond to you in such a way—the way you experienced everyone else responding."

"No, it was what I expected. It's what I would always provoke in others. I think that was the point."

"A self-fulfilling prophecy?" I suggested. "People judged you because they were fearful of your criticism?"

"Exactly," he agreed. "And I could then feel justified in my criticism. It was a perfect vicious circle but I think I've finally broken it. But what were you fearful of when you first met me?"

After some consideration I said, "I think I too feared you would find fault with me, that you would complain about me in the scathing way you complained of others."

"Oh, I did," said Victor candidly. "I told Margaret what a hopeless therapist you were and, of course, it was her fault for sending me to you!"

"And yet you continued with me," I observed. "What was it that kept you coming here?"

Now Victor took some moments to consider his response. "This may sound odd," he said. "But do you remember when I asked if you saw me as a hopeless case?"

"I do," I answered. "I said you hadn't presented yourself as a case to be hopeless about."

"That's right, but you said something before that," he said.

"Did I? I don't remember." I replied honestly, puzzled as to what I could have said that had made him stay.

"The very first thing you said was, 'No, I don't think that at all'," he explained. "And though you went on to say that I didn't have a case—that I saw the case as the world rather than myself—and though I knew you didn't completely believe what you had said, those words stayed with me. Whether you knew it or not, whether you believed it fully or not, what I heard, perhaps selectively, was 'You are not a hopeless case'."

"So though you thought I was a hopeless therapist, that's what kept you coming?" I asked in amazement.

"Yes," he replied. "It's what I needed to believe."

I'm tempted to end this account of therapy with Victor at this point. It would be such a good place to stop—a happy ending is always so appealing and it would leave me fairly sure I'd presented myself as not too bad a therapist (at least by the end, and despite my initial judgemental and unempathic response). I might even have convinced myself of my earlier claim that maybe I'm "a competent couple therapist when working with individuals". But then, however much we might like to think the opposite, life and therapy are unpredictable and I think I should be honest enough to tell the whole story.

It was not long after that moving session in which we both authentically responded to each other, intimate in our confession of our experience of each other and appreciative of the work we'd done together, that Victor, on his return from the summer break, dropped the bombshell. Margaret, accusing him of acting the happy husband "too cocky for words", and being "bored to death" by his new benign attentiveness, had thrown him out. I mean, physically and violently thrown him out. He had the bruises to prove it.

Now, I'm not one to believe that even good couple therapy is all about keeping couples together. Often enough, the inevitable and only outcome is to recognise the irreparable incompatibility of the couple and for them to part, hopefully amicably, using the therapy to support each other in their separation. Sadly, this was not going to be the case with Victor and Margaret. It was finished. She wanted nothing more to do with him. No pleading, no suggestion of couple therapy, no negotiation was allowed. He was out on his ear and living in a bedsit pending further developments, namely getting some money from the house, which Margaret was steadfastly refusing to leave.

Victor is devastated. I wouldn't blame him if he reverted to his former endless complaining—about Margaret, about me, about therapy, about the world. But he doesn't. He continues to come week after week, sobs for most of the session and, when not in tears, attempts to get some understanding of what he's done wrong. I feel like saying, "It's not you Victor, it's her, it's life!" but I don't want to undo all the work we've been doing and risk reinforcing his one-time perception of the world as totally negative and threatening—though right now, in relation to what's happened to him, I'm beginning to have my doubts.

I know "shit happens"—but why now? Why to poor Victor? It seems so unfair, and, yes, I can hear myself explaining to my clients that life has nothing to do with fairness or unfairness, it just is, and it's impartial to what happens to us mere mortals— but this is all sounding rather hollow and platitudinous to me even as I think it. Ironically, it's me that wants to play *"Ain't it awful?"* and *"If it weren't for her"*, even *"You always, she never"*. I'm certainly hearing *"I should have listened to my client"* reverberating loudly in my head as I remember Victor's warning words describing his wife, with absolute conviction, as sadomasochistic. How right he has turned out to be.

In the changed circumstances, missing the former persecution by the miserable victim Victor, Margaret had no use for him. The disappearance of her foil in the whole sadist/masochist drama that was their relationship left her bereft and furious like an addict without her fix. Now that he had become a benign, delightful and confident man he was not what she needed so she'd spat him out.

My newly coined Meldroid personality disorder with its seemingly innocuous and slightly comical sadomasochistic elements has proved inept. In fact, it's a totally crass and useless diagnostic category. It appears so trite and stupid in retrospect as I continue to work as best I can with this broken man. And though my decision not to work with couples remains intact, I've surely learnt the lesson about taking sides in relationships, even with individual clients. Except that, right now, I'm totally, fairly and squarely on Victor's side and solidly against that dreadful, despicable Margaret.

Woody Bay

We sit in silence for some time as we have done quite frequently. It's comfortable. There's no urgency to fill the space, no sense of time being wasted. Rather, we bask in the passing moments and find solace there. Even Emily's slightly laboured breathing seems to contribute a meditative rhythm to our shared reverie. My chest rises and falls in unison with her breath. Time passes and yet stands still.

Emily is dying. For three years, despite knowing the poor prognosis for someone in her eighties, she underwent the toxic invasion of chemotherapy. Following several periods of treatment, remission and relapse, she resigned herself to living with cancer and two years ago came into therapy with me to support her in "living towards death" as she put it. Having never drunk, smoked or taken drugs in her eighty-seven years, she is now dependent on morphine for pain relief. Yet, with a glint in her eye, she refers to herself as a "late-blooming smack head", with no complaint of unfairness at her fate.

I notice the late afternoon sun shining on her head, the almost perfect yellow-pink dome of which is clearly visible beneath the few remaining wisps of white hair. If I were to touch the top of her head, her downy hair would be barely perceptible, like a light breath against my skin. I imagine letting the tips of my fingers gently trace the contours of her head. The words *pass your hand over my brow* come into my mind; the first line of a poem I once knew so well but struggle to remember now. Something about feeling where the brain grows. I think of Emily's dying brain, of the innumerable memories stored there, though some, the more recent ones, are lost to her conscious attention; lost like the poem is to me. I wish I could remember it. It has a line about being like a tree and seeing footprints leading up to it and I think Emily would appreciate it.

"I'm thinking of Woody Bay," she says softly, as if not to disturb the silence too much. "And you?" she asks.

"Also trees," I reply. I make no remark about the synchronicity: such things happen so often between Emily and me that they've become commonplace, without need of mention. "Trees as a metaphor for life," I say. "Do you want to tell me about Woody Bay?"

"I'm sure I must have told you before," she says smiling.

"Maybe," I say, returning her smile.

"There's nothing worse than an old woman wittering on repeatedly about the past like a broken record. You must stop me if I have," she insists.

"Maybe," I say again, knowing I have no intention of stopping her.

"It's a good metaphor for human life, the tree," she continues. "After years of growth through the changing seasons, they die of old age or disease just like us."

"That's true," I say.

She does not say more. As the lowering sun reddens the sky, the room is bathed in a soft, warm light. She closes her eyes and we sit again in silence for a while. I think she is asleep but it is hard to tell. Her waking state is sometimes so ethereal I don't know which of us may be asleep and dreaming, or awake and still dreaming, or dreaming that we are awake. I think of my grandmother and the hours I spent as a child sitting with her in a similar timelessness. It was a long time ago but I feel the warmth of her still. Emily has the same soft, enveloping quality, like the warm sun playing upon her head as it drops forward slightly. She is stirred by this involuntary movement and raises her eyes to mine.

"It was a long time ago," she says.

"Woody Bay?" I enquire.

"Yes, I'm still there," she acknowledges.

"It was a long time ago," I repeat, not knowing quite why I'm emphasising this fact (though my own "long time ago" thought is still somewhere in my mind). She knows it only too well, has told me before that it feels like another lifetime, another world ago, even another person ago. Yet it is always so present.

"I was thirteen, I think, maybe fourteen-years-old," she says. Her age has changed. She was slightly older last time but it is no matter. It is her memory to do with as she wishes, although I suspect wishing has little moment against the erosion of her mind.

"And you're still there," I say.

"Well, like young people today might say, 'I wish!'" she chuckles loudly yet somewhat wistfully. The phrase sounds incongruous on her elderly lips but she is clearly amused by such modern idioms. She has spoken before of her desire to keep abreast of the world she will soon leave. But I know her earlier world holds even more importance for her despite the fullness of the life she has lived since.

"What are you doing there?" I ask, taking her back to it and, at the same time, wondering if it's right to ask her something I already know; something she does not remember having told me. It feels disingenuous of me, like I'm playing some sort of game with reality.

"I've walked over from the farmhouse," she replies. I know this to be the farm in Martinhoe in north Devon, the place to which she was evacuated. Her parents remained in London where, along with 40,000 other civilians, they were shortly to be killed in the Blitz. She always wondered if her father might have survived if he'd been called up rather than continuing his work on the railways. She knew it was a pointless wonder.

"It's a beautiful day," continues Emily, at least, I assume she continues and is not referring to today as she stares out of the window at the late sun. "They're oaks, you know, covering the steep hillside right down to the sea. I love that, trees and sea, green on blue, land and sea and sky—my perfect landscape. The sun is high in a clear sky and dappling the grassy path that winds down between the tall trees. I always remember Virginia Woolf's description—'Islands of light are swimming on the grass, they have fallen through the trees'."

She pauses, no doubt seeing those sunny islands in her mind's eye. "I run down some of the way, but where it's most steep, I walk, almost crouching, digging my heels into the soft peat. The smell is a rich, heady mixture of salt and rich earth and, I don't know, could it be rhododendrons?" She inhales through her nose as if to discover an answer. I find myself sniffing too and catch the very present scent of the honeysuckle that tangles beneath the window. I smile at my failed attempt to join her in Woody Bay, but she is not there either. "Could having children have helped?" she asks.

"Helped in what way?" I enquire, following her apparent non sequitur.

"Oh, maybe to feel more fulfilled, to have left something good behind," she suggests with a long sigh. Her head falls forward again but this time into sleep, not out of it.

I sit silently. I think of all the good Emily has done in her life, and the good that will continue after her death. When still a young woman, she had trained as a children's nurse but soon became attracted to working solely with troubled children (she hated the term "maladjusted" and only just tolerated "children with special needs"). She retrained as a teacher, and many schools and special units owe their existence today to her pioneering work in the field.

She believed a child's world could be opened up and transformed through education within a therapeutic milieu; that even the most troubled child's behaviour could be changed through learning—in particular, through learning to read (later research was to prove her right). She devised reading schemes aimed at children for whom the orderly, middle-class lives of "Janet and John" had no relevance, let alone interest. She helped thousands of troubled children.

The sun is shining higher now upon the white wall behind her, on the lamps and on the impressionistic painting of a landscape, but her face is illuminated still in the soft light. I notice the deep lines that her kindness has left etched across her brow, upon her cheeks and round her mouth: lines of caring and laughter. And, in between these furrows, islands again, long strands of loosened skin that tell of loss and longing, of times when perhaps her caring would have been better directed towards herself—or requested from another.

She has led a selfless life, a giving life. She has made life work out for others in a way that it did not work out for her. Perhaps the two are inextricably linked. I watch her sleeping peacefully, sad to think she may not fully know the impact she has had upon the world, the invaluable legacy she is leaving. I wonder if the handing down of biological genes in a few offspring would have matched the incredible and continuing importance of her work for many generations of children. Perhaps it is the proximity, the close continuity, the intermingling of our identities with our own children that leaves us feeling we have influence; that we are leaving something of ourselves behind, something good, something worthwhile. I question this. I question whether Emily could have done both. Might not one have diluted, if not badly diminished, the other?

She stirs and focuses immediately out of the window and across the valley. As always, I do not feel ignored but included in her gaze, as if she takes me with her. "You have more elms here," she observes, and, not waiting for me to comment, continues, "I think perhaps it *is* the smell of rhododendrons. There's a big house further up. They probably have them in their grounds. The mix of sweetness and earthiness could almost make you faint—heavenly!" Descriptively appropriate though it may be, I'm struck by her choice of exclamation. It's not a word she's used before nor does it sound quite congruent on the lips of a defiant atheist. It seems she has the same thought. "I'm not having a deathbed conversion!" she laughs, lifting her feet from the floor. "It's a fine word but I don't expect heaven when I've fallen off my perch. I won't be savouring any smells come the day!"

"You read my mind too well," I say, smiling with her. "As you say, it's a fine word, even if an unusual one for you to use."

"Heavenly," she says once more and pauses again to recall the fragrance. A lone tear rolls down her cheek. I begin to doubt the usefulness of this particular reminiscence. I question why I have encouraged her. Would it not be better to turn elsewhere, to count her achievements, to look back at her subsequent, successful life? I hope she might simply go off at some other tangent, as she is wont to do. Her eyes close. Perhaps she is sleeping again. But no, "He's standing under the waterfall," she says, and I know it is too late. She will stay with the story to its end. Maybe this is right. Maybe this is what she needs to do—has to do, at least one more time.

"He doesn't see me sitting under the arch of the lime kiln in the lee of the rocks. He's standing almost naked under the waterfall, lifting his face to the torrent and letting the icy water splash upon his lithe, beautiful body. He's oblivious to being observed at all, he's so lost in his ablution. I'm fascinated by him, by the whole unexpected scenario, and embarrassed too—not by his nakedness but to be invading his privacy in this way. But my fascination wins and I can't look away. I think his face seems familiar. I wonder if he's a labourer from a neighbouring farm, or maybe one of the young fishermen from Lynmouth who's avoided being called up as yet. But I can't place him at all and I realise his familiarity isn't actual, it's what I've wish for. Isn't it crazy—a young girl seeing a boy on a beach and falling in love before she's even met him?"

"But that's how it was," I assure her. "That's how you felt. Young love can be like that. It can take you by surprise."

"It is such a surprise, a shock even," she continues. "My whole body trembles, my heart races ... all the clichés! There's a longing in me that I've never experienced before, not even missing my parents. It's inexplicable, but all I know is that I'm enchanted and I want to be with him."

I feel like I'm sitting on some other rock on that beach, observing Emily observing the youth under the waterfall. As she speaks, the collected decades have melted from her face. She is the young, beautiful girl sitting in the sun on Woody Bay. I feel her youthful passion rising in her like an unstoppable force, the same unstoppable, passionate force that was to propel her into her life's work.

"He's drying his hair with his singlet. I can see now that, in the drying, what before had looked like dark hair is short and blond. He looks up and sees me watching and stops his rubbing. There's a pause, a fleeting moment's shyness before he smiles at me. I like that, the shyness and the smile; they suggest a tender sensitivity. It gives me the confidence to return his smile but I'm not sure what to do next. Luckily, he doesn't wait for me to make that decision. He treads his way carefully across the grey stones towards his clothes piled like a pillow on a flat, sloping rock where he'd clearly been sunbathing. Once there, his smile never leaving his face, he beckons me with an eager gesture of his hand to join him."

She pauses again. Her eyes are closed. Her breathing has become more laboured and I wonder if she is in physical pain. I ask if she needs the morphine that she carries with her all the time now, but she shakes her head. "No, I'm thinking of 'stranger danger'," she says, bringing herself out of her remembered past.

"I've argued vehemently against its overemphasis in schools. There's more of a danger that we're encouraging mistrust in a world where we badly need to trust. It can feel like everyone is out to do us harm. It's not the rare predatory stranger who needs to overly concern us, it's nearer to home. It's the relatives we should worry about. They're invariably the abusers, hidden in the seclusion of their homes. Sadly, I've seen it so often. I wonder, had 'stranger danger' been around as strongly in those long-ago days, perhaps I wouldn't have responded to his beckoning, maybe I'd rather have—what's the phrase?—'hot-footed it' back up the hill. But I didn't. I don't. I respond to his open smile and I trust him. I pick my way over the rocks to where he sits like a merman by a pool. I boldly say 'hello' and even more boldly sit by his side without waiting for an answer. I can feel the cool of his body chilled by the waterfall and I sit close, but without touching, in the hope that the heat of my sun-baked body will warm him. And when he returns my 'hello' in a German accent, I feel no surprise or fear or disappointment, simply curiosity. What on earth is he doing here on the beach at Woody Bay?"

Emily stops, puts her head on one side like a sparrow. I wonder if this is the movement that accompanied her curiosity on the rocks. "You know my family originates from Germany?" she asks. I tell her I do. "It's ironic, isn't it, that my parents were killed in England? They thought they were safe here, it was so much their home." Another pause, a bewildered expression on her face. "Why am I telling you about my parents?"

"You were talking about Walther," I say, realising I've called him by his name. She doesn't seem to notice her omission of his name so far today, or question how I come to know it. It doesn't seem to matter. Maybe she knows she has told me this story several times, and that doesn't matter either. I hope she knows I don't simply tolerate her repetition, but welcome it like a returning friend who, changing imperceptibly each time, keeps the familiarity and the meaning alive through those subtle alterations. "But do you want to talk of your parents?" I ask, already knowing that in all likelihood she does not. She ignores my question.

"His English is perfectly understandable and I have quite a good grasp of German to assist us when he falters. In any case, language is not our main means of communication that day, though we talk with ease. We talk as if we are old friends. But mostly it is our faces that are speaking, and our bodies sending signals. The words are simply an extraneous formality. There is no war in our world at this moment. Even when he tells me of his U-boat out in the channel, so near to our shore, it doesn't sound sinister from his smiling mouth. He explains that he and his fellow soldiers have been playing football not far away, further down at Heddon Mouth, and bathing, larking about, collecting fresh water. It all seems so normal, so ordinary. Somehow I feel oddly elated that the secluded shores of Exmoor provide peace so indiscriminately, especially for Walther and me. Here on our rock by the sea, we are an amnesty that could end the war, if only others could feel it too."

I watch her tears well and fall. She looks ecstatic in her visionary state where the world, if only it could experience her and Walther's serenity, would be at peace. I feel, as I have felt before in the presence of this woman and her story, a faint jealousy. I have not experienced such a connection, so instant, so innocent and trusting. It is a lack I carry with me like a deep longing. In her place, I may have watched from the lime kiln, may have adored from afar, but soon I would have made for the oak wood armed only with brave and excited fantasies of meeting, of invented, intricate conversation, of what might have been. "I've never told anyone of Walther," she informs me, again. "I can tell you because I know you must have heard so many crazy stories, perhaps some crazier than mine."

"Why crazy?" I ask.

"Because, looking back, I suspect it was a madness, a delusion. What might you call it—a 'folie à deux'?"

"I don't think so," I reply. "You were strangers. For both of you to simultaneously develop the same delusion is more like a miracle than a madness!"

"Whatever," she says dismissively, almost but not quite in the manner au courant (she could never sound surly enough for that). "I'm not sure anyone would believe that two young people could meet and fall in love in an instant, and stay in love forever."

"But you did. You have," I insist, aware that I want it to be so, want this dying woman to hold on to her memory of young love. Or is this solely a need in me? Is this my own longing rather than an altruistic wish for Emily? I'm not sure, and maybe I cannot know.

"We did, I have," she says with conviction. "We talk and laugh and share our hopes. I learn nothing of his history, nor he of mine. It feels like our lives start here, the past is irrelevant and forgotten, everything is timeless and now. But, of course, we cannot really escape time and necessity. The sun is lowering and eventually he must go to rejoin his fellow soldiers, and I too must return to my billet."

I notice the present sun has lowered too. The room has dimmed and flattened, lacking the sharp edge of shadows. I look at Emily in this diffuse light, concerned that she looks so tired. I suggest she might need to finish telling her story at this juncture, even before her hour is up, that she could simply rest and we could wait quietly together for her carer to arrive.

Again, I wonder if this is the part of the story I want her to stay with, those happy hours with Walther before they have to part. Perhaps I have some romantic notion of a deathbed scene in which our suffering and regrets are lost to recollection and solely the ecstasies of our past are relived in our last few moments. But Emily, despite her experience of this epitome of a romantic encounter, is far more pragmatic. I can tell from her shift in posture, raising herself more upright, placing her feet more squarely on the floor, that she is not going to leave it there.

"We don't make love," she announces as if I'd made that assumption. "I want to … I so want to. And I now regret that we didn't. But Walther is such a gentleman. He's so concerned he might be taking advantage that he wants us to wait. I don't think for one minute he has doubts. He is quite sure we'll be together after the war—in what, a few months' time? Oh, how naive we are! In the meantime, expecting his submarine to remain in the channel a while longer, we will meet again on the beach. Of course, he cannot know exactly when he might return but I will come to the beach each day, and one day he will be there. There is no doubt about that for either of us. We enfold each other close as we say goodbye. It's an embrace more magical than the one I'd so instantly craved as I watched him under the waterfall." She sobs. Knowing how the story ends, I am relieved she grieves so openly, though I know her grief will accompany her to the end.

I am perhaps not the Pollyanna I make myself out to be. I know most theories of mourning would argue that over time our grief will end, our loss be integrated. But why should losses fade with time? Why should the gaping holes left by dead friends be any less tomorrow than they are today? Life is changed. It can never be the same. We may walk along in a different world quite well, even happily at times, but the voids are with us. They are holes in our very being.

"It was thought to be a naval mine," she says, and I notice her change of tense. I surmise, by so doing, she is protecting herself from the full impact. "I don't know how many days or weeks I continued to stand on the rock by the pool staring out to sea, but when I heard that a Nazi submarine had been holed in the channel, been sunk, destroyed, exploded, annihilated, dealt with—various euphemisms were used that made no mention of people, just the craft—I knew that Walther was dead. He had been violently killed, that gentle young man, and I had been holed, sunk, destroyed—all those words describe how I felt. It's how I still feel. What I wouldn't give to have that day in Woody Bay again. Given a second chance, I would make love with him and not say goodbye. We would hide until the war is over and raise our family. I think I would have been a good mother to our children. I think we would have been happy."

I hesitate to speak. I want to tell her that she has been a good mother to so many children throughout her long and influential life, that her love for Walther has been so generously dispersed among generations of troubled children that he lives on in them, that … but I know this sentiment is not the reality. Her successful work, her purposeful life, has simply been a second best; a poor substitute for what might have been. Of course, it is useless and foolish to say "If only …" but it is very human. I say nothing.

She is leaving now. I notice how frail she is, how her back is bent forward and her thin arms barely able to take her weight on her walking sticks as her young carer supports her to the door. "I'll see you next week," I say, though I'm not so sure.

"Maybe," says Emily, sounding equally uncertain. "Thank you for today. Thank you for taking me back to Woody Bay."

"It's been a pleasure," I say with absolute certainty.

Super vision

"If Sophie was an animal, what would she be?" asked my supervisor before I'd given any details beyond my client's name. This exercise was one Christine often used when I introduced a new client in supervision. Actually, Sophie had been with me for some months; it was just that so far I hadn't found immediate cause to present her. Other clients had pressed preferentially for time and attention by the greater degree of difficulty I was experiencing with them. Perhaps this said something about Sophie. She was so undemanding in life, she could easily get overlooked. I didn't want that to happen in our work, and while she would never know if I discussed her with my supervisor or not, *I* would know and I was sure that this could affect our work together, however subtly.

Guessing that Christine was likely to employ this technique, I'd come prepared. I'd even thought of Sophie as a type of flower, a tree, a mode of transport, a colour and a building, just in case. Trying to sound spontaneous, I answered instantly, "A wren."

"Now let another animal come into your mind," instructed Christine. Maybe she thought a bird didn't really count.

"A startled rabbit," I replied, describing the image that had now appeared in my mind unbidden. Christine closed her eyes. "And another adjective?"

"Hesitant," I added immediately. "A hesitant, startled rabbit."

"And if you put her in a scenario, where is she?"

I did not have to think twice. I could see her there. "She's at the roadside."

"What sort of road?" asked Christine, seeing the detail as important to the exercise.

"A country lane," I said. "She's crouched on the verge. She can see other rabbits in a field on the other side nibbling some sweet grasses ... but she's too frightened to hop across the road." Christine opened her eyes and looked at me quizzically. "She's had problems on the road before?"

"I'm not sure, but her mother has told her how dangerous they are, even quiet country lanes. She knows a car could come zooming along out of control at any moment."

"So she's understandably hesitant," said Christine softly. "But startled? Why is she startled? Has something already happened?"

"I don't know," I said, then changed my mind. "I think maybe she can hear a car. I think the engine has backfired and startled her. Or it might have been gunshots. Nothing nearby but she's heard a loud noise."

"Put yourself in the scene," directed Christine, leaning forward as if to join me, resting her folded arms on her knee. "How are you going to help her? What do think you will do?"

"I'll move very slowly," I said. "I don't want to frighten her. And then ... um ... and then ..."

"Don't let judgements get in the way, just go with it," advised Christine reading my mind. "Here's a startled rabbit, hesitant to cross the road to get to her fellow creatures and the sweet grass, and you've crept up to her slowly and carefully so as not to frighten her. What then?"

"I pick her up and cradle her in my arms," I said, feeling uncomfortable, as Christine had probably surmised, that this might sound rather schmaltzy, and questionable. I plunged on regardless. "I cradle her in my arms and I stroke her to calm her and I carry her across the road to safety with the other rabbits."

"And the grass," added Christine. "Don't forget the sweet grass."

"Ah, yes," I agreed. "There's the sweet grass."

"And then?"

"I wait with her until I feel it's safe to leave her with the other rabbits," I said, picturing myself sitting on a mossy bank watching her. "Then I walk away slowly."

"That sounds like a happy ending!" smiled Christine, settling back in her chair and writing something in her notebook. "And just before you dismiss it as some silly fairy story, remember it's not just clients' expectations that affect the outcome of psychotherapy, it's the therapist's too." The idea made sense to me. It was certainly suggested by research findings in teacher expectations of pupils, though whether there was any research to this effect in the psychotherapy field, I didn't know. It seemed highly likely that the principle would apply here equally.

"So what might we understand of Sophie from this?" came Christine's next, predictable words. "Equally, what can we understand about your relationship to Sophie from this? You were evidently very uncomfortable at one stage."

So that was the point we went in on: my unease when I'd talked about picking her up and cradling her. Was it my fear of this being seen as sexual? The bit about stroking her could easily have such a connotation but I thought not. Did I feel shame at the thought of cradling her, of stroking her? Well, yes and no. In the fantasy, no, I'd feel fine about soothing a rabbit in this way. But I had felt not shame exactly, but embarrassment when I was aware of Christine listening. I'd come out of the fantasy at that point, conscious of being watched, then self-conscious of what I'd said and how it might sound. It wasn't the sexual angle but more to do with me being judged. I could be accused of gratifying my client automatically, of rescuing her rather than letting her find her own way (across the road and in life).

"For the moment, if you put aside your reason for feeling self-conscious, which, of course, is your own internal critic rather than anything to do with me," went on Christine (I hoped her tongue was partly in her cheek as she said this). "Where's the human Sophie in this enactment?"

"Being watched vigilantly by her mother," I suggested, knowing only too well about Sophie's mother and her overwhelming tightness of control.

"And not in a caring way, I suspect," said Christine.

"No, she's looking out for anything in Sophie that she can criticise and scold her for."

"So Sophie will be anxious that you will do the same," she proposed. She waited for my nod of assent before adding, "Like you thought I was with you."

"I guess," I admitted reluctantly.

"There may be a *tiny* grain of truth in the latter," added Christine with a smile. "You do have a tendency to rescue at times … but back to Sophie and her obsessive compulsions."

"What?" I exclaimed, knowing I hadn't mentioned anything of the sort. "How …?"

Christine smiled wryly. "Think about what you've just told me."

"You mean her mother being vigilant, critical, and sadistic? That's not enough. Not everyone with that type of mother turns out to be obsessive compulsive," I asserted, sounding a bit defensive.

"No, you're right," said Christine. "But they'd certainly be extremely anxious—just like hesitant and startled rabbits.

And her mother put the fear of god into her—it was probably her own anxiety. She's made her terrified of quiet country lanes, for which read 'life'. You know, I think it's rare for out-of-control cars to come zooming along quiet country lanes. It would have been enough just to say 'take care'. This mother creates anxiety by the bucket load."

"OK," I replied, appeased by her earlier affirmation, and impressed by her discerning insight. She'd got Sophie's mother to a tee. "But how did you get from that to obsessive compulsive?"

"It wasn't so much the story as your behaviour," explained Christine. "A bit of a giveaway really."

I carefully sat still. "Oh yes, so what was I doing?"

"Being very un-Michael," she said. "You don't usually sit so primly—in fact, you usually slouch terribly, and I still hope you'll sort that out one day, but you sat upright. Your feet and knees were perfectly together, and throughout most of the story you kept checking that the buttons on your shirt were straight. You even picked off non-existent lint from your trousers."

"I was being Sophie," I agreed. "That's exactly how she behaves in the sessions."

"Amazing, isn't it, the power of unconscious process?"

"It sure is," I said. "Even when we know about it, we can't avoid it."

"And her mother is dead, I take it?" advanced Christine from left field, again taking me by surprise.

"She is," I said matter-of-factly. I didn't want to ask her how she knew. I thought she was being too clever by half already. But she told me anyway.

"Bit of a guess actually but there was something about the car backfiring or the gunshots ... all in the distance (you made a point of saying 'not nearby') and I thought at the time these loud noises might be from beyond the grave—the mother in her head."

"A very loud voice in her head," I concurred.

"And dad?" asked Christine. Churlishly, I felt pleased she hadn't also guessed about him. Not that there was much to guess.

"I don't know much about him yet," I confessed. "Army man, not around much, never has been." Christine lifted her eyes and met my gaze. "Mm, distant gunshots … abandoned, anxious wife … danger, things out of control. Anyway, tell me more about Sophie, the only child. We can come back to the rabbit story later." I didn't even go near her accurate "only child" deduction.

More sensitised as a result of the exercise, I realised just how emotionally and psychologically traumatising Sophie's childhood had been. I was glad I'd brought her to supervision today, but I was critical of myself for not bringing her even sooner. I'd underestimated the degree of damage Sophie had suffered and continued to suffer as an adult. Easy to overlook in the undemanding quietness of her anxiety, I'd unfortunately done exactly that by giving preference to my other, louder clients. Perhaps, like her father, I'd neglected to fully be with her. I shared my self-criticism with Christine, who simply and kindly said she understood how this can happen in a busy practice. I appreciated her acceptance and observed it was a far cry from how Sophie's mother would have reacted. "So start there," she said, finding a way in.

I told her I'd never heard such an awful and damning curse from anyone, let alone from a mother to her child, but Sophie's mother had inflicted it upon Sophie on a daily basis. Vigilant for any excuse to cruelly admonish Sophie (it could be as small as an untied shoelace), she would scream and shout and shake Sophie like a rag doll. But this was not the worst of it. Sophie, terrified and tearful, could only think to say, "I love you mummy." Then would come the ubiquitous damning curse, "Well, I don't love you, nobody loves you, and no one ever will!" I said the words in the venomous tone I'd inferred from Sophie's lower-keyed imitation of her mother and I could see Christine's startled expression as I said them. Not one to blaspheme, Christine's "Jesus wept!" came as a surprise. But then, with moist eyes and a quieter voice, she declared, "That is wicked. That is truly cruel. I'm so sorry." I felt like she was talking to me.

Sophie's obsessions and compulsions had started at a very early age. She had few toys, little company and sparse attention except of the negative type, so alone in her bedroom, she would stare for hours at the ceiling, attempting to work her way from one corner to another along the interweaving cracks without coming to a dead end. She'd told me she never quite made it and had to start again each time. Another similar "game" when she was a bit older was to walk across the carpet with its swirly pattern of multiple beiges, seeing if she could get to the other side on a particular shade of brown in a number of steps that had to be divisible by a number she had arbitrarily chosen at the beginning. It sounded tortuous to me, empty and deadening.

Christine concurred. "But what do you make of them, these rituals? To Sophie they must have been vital. What purpose do you think they served for her?"

I'd pondered their purpose a great deal over the preceding months. "I think they served, still serve, multiple purposes."

"Yes, probably," she agreed.

"Some sense of structure for one thing, structure of time and space, something she'd created for herself rather than it being imposed upon her," I mused. "In that precarious, irrational environment she must have felt so unsafe. Perhaps these repetitive rituals and patterns provided something logical to her, something that followed familiar rules, something unthreatening."

Christine nodded slowly. I'd noticed all her movements had slowed down. Even her speech had become soft and slow, like she was creeping up on a startled rabbit.

55

"What form do they take now?" she asked, and I rattled off the more common ones such as checking taps and light switches, ruminating over minor problems like whether she'd paid the gas bill or put the rubbish out, tidying incessantly. The more disruptive ones—the ones that took more time and effort and made her life more dysfunctional—were rituals like "having to" count things—curtain rings, cracks in the pavement, railings—before she could proceed to do whatever she was meant to be doing.

But the most disturbing and troublesome was a fear when driving that she'd run someone over. When she had this thought, she would have to stop, inspect the car (looking for blood), and scour the vicinity for any signs of a body. She never found one but this was not the end of it. Back home, usually in the middle of the night, she would realise there was a shrub she hadn't searched thoroughly enough or imagine that she hadn't killed the person outright and that they'd managed to drag themselves further afield where she hadn't looked. She had to go back. No matter the time or how far away the imagined accident had occurred, she had to return to the scene, sometimes two or three times the same night.

Luckily she was self-employed and did her graphic design work from home, otherwise she would have lost her job long before now. But, often exhausted by the night's activities, her creativity and productivity suffered enormously. There was always something she had to count, check, recheck, and watch out for. It was a relentless round that never got her anywhere but back to the beginning.

"I'm reminded of your fantasy," put in Christine, having heard the litany of varying obsessions and compulsions. "She doesn't get to the other side of the road until you help her. If you hadn't entered the scene, she'd still be at the roadside, probably counting blades of grass or how many rabbits are on the other side where she so wants to be."

"I think coming into therapy with me is the first time she's asked for help," I observed. "She wants me to help her to deal with the rituals so she can get on with her life more healthily."

Christine settled back in her chair. "But you won't do that will you?"

For a moment I wondered what she meant, thinking she was saying there was no way I could help her, but she explained without my asking. "In the fantasy you don't deal with any rituals. You don't even notice whether she has any or not—that was my surmising. You don't try to change her behaviour at all; you help her in a different way." The penny was dropping. Christine was making conscious a useful rule of thumb when working with people who have an obsessive-compulsive way of being: address their obsessive thinking, aim for their feelings, avoid their compulsive behaviour that will in all likelihood change eventually as their thoughts and feelings change. Giving attention to the behaviour, making it a focus too soon, can lead to disappointment as the behaviour continues—or worse, can have the effect of escalating it to an even higher level.

"But I went in on her feelings," I confessed. "I didn't address her thinking."

"And you speak rabbit do you?" came Christine's amused repost. "I'm sure if you did, you'd have been talking with her about the very unhelpful stuff going on in her head. As it is, you don't speak rabbit, so you sensibly went straight for her feelings of anxiety."

The theory wasn't quite fitting with the story, and I wondered if Christine was a bit put out by my highlighting this lack of neatness. I even wondered if she was rescuing me (which would have been very unusual) in describing my intervention as sensible. However, she seemed quite at ease with it all and, untidy though it may have been, I was grateful she'd reminded me of it.

I was aware that at times in our sessions I *had* focused on Sophie's behaviour and had even suggested some alternative ways of dealing with it. This approach had luckily not worsened her compulsions but it had gone nowhere, so it was helpful to have a perspective as to why it had been ineffective. I was making a mental note to be more aware of this when Christine remarked, "You know, don't you, that all the buttons on your shirt don't have to be straight?" She was, of course, talking to me and to Sophie. I heard it for both of us.

I revealed more of Sophie's history, her early years, her school experiences, her adult years, and the desperate anxiety that permeated her life. I described the touching ritual she had devised when she was four, when she felt the whole world was crashing in on her, in which she would crouch down and repeat the mantra, "I'm not going to worry, worry-worry-worry, I'm not going to worry anymore, from … now!" at which point she would leap into the air feeling free of it. But it did not last long. Sometimes only a few moments later she would be crouching again, repeating her incantation even though the gods were clearly not listening. "It was, is, all so futile," was Christine's sad response. "But she has a chance with you."

"I hope so," I replied, touched by her words. I looked at her enquiringly.

"It's in your story, isn't it, the chance she has with you?" she went on, as if in answer to my look. "I know you're not going to actually cradle her and stroke her, as you did the rabbit, but I think your story showed how you recognise that those obsessional thoughts and futile rituals are her way of doing just that. She's trying to regulate her emotions—especially her terror and anxiety—in her repetitions, her familiar patterns, her search for a way across the ceiling, the carpet, across the road. She's trying to provide what her mother badly failed to provide her with."

"Yes, I think she is," I acknowledged. "I think she's trying to soothe herself—but it doesn't last."

"No," agreed Christine. "There isn't as yet an internalised other to hold onto it. But what a brave attempt." I felt tearful in response. A sigh was all I could manage.

Christine changed gear. "So?"

"So?"

"Does your story help to find a better and hopefully more permanent way?" she asked. "Where does your fantasy take her?"

"Ah, the sweet grass," I replied, my sadness lifting for now. "And the other rabbits."

"And what do they mean to you?"

"Nourishment," I suggested. "Contact … relationship … safety."

"Mm," mused Christine. "Psychotherapy then."

"Oh that," I smiled.

"But slowly, very slowly," added Christine. "I think you'll be on that road for a long time, calming her, soothing her until she can do that for herself and get herself across to the other side. I imagine you'll be bringing her here quite often. Now, did you have someone else you wanted to bring? You were a bit stuck with your macho man with erectile dysfunction a few weeks ago. How's he doing?"

But I wasn't quite ready to move on from Sophie. There was something niggling me about the way we'd started the story-telling, the very first part of it.

"I'm wondering about the wren," I said. "I mean, what if we'd stayed with Sophie as a wren rather than a rabbit?"

Christine was already putting her notes about Sophie away in a file. "What about it?"

"Well, would the story have illuminated the same aspects as the rabbit story?" I enquired. "Would we have come to where we are now?"

Christine did not hesitate. "No, not with the wren, I'm absolutely sure we wouldn't."

"So what's the point?" I objected. "What's the point if it's different every time according to which animal we choose?"

"Did I say that?"

"More or less."

"No I didn't" she insisted. "I said not with the wren."

I thought she was being unnecessarily pedantic. "What's wrong with a wren?" I exclaimed, sounding, I'm sure, as exasperated with her as I felt. Christine calmly opened her notepad at a new page. "Nothing wrong with a spontaneous wren ... nothing at all ... but a rehearsed wren? Well, apart from cheating, it's just not going to work at all."

Different again

It felt odd calling him Junior given he was in his late 50s and not diminutive in any way, shape, or form. He was the tallest and most muscular man I'd ever met and intimidating simply by being the mass that he was. Despite his physical presence, anyone less imposing was hard to imagine. He spoke with a soft, lilting voice that was reassuring and mesmeric, his Jamaican patois and inflection noticeable only occasionally when it punctuated his educated, received pronunciation. On the phone I hadn't picked up on this slight intonation and I'd imagined him to be white. On meeting with him in person I asked him straight off how it might be for him to work with a white therapist.

"Dat's why mi deh yah," he sang, seeming to deliberately emphasise the patois before reverting to RP. "You have to be white to help me with my issue."

My curiosity was instantly aroused. "And that is?" I asked.

"Racism," he replied.

"Ah," I said, words failing me for a moment as I tried to get my head around what he might be meaning and how therapy might help. I thought it easiest just to ask.

"I mean, I want to work out how to deal with racism," he explained in reply. "It's not something I'm unfamiliar with, as

61

you might imagine, but I hadn't expected it on the course I'm doing and I need to find a way to deal with it."

"And the course you are doing is …?"

"I'm training to be a psychotherapist."

"Ah," I said a second time, this time because there were too many words to get my head around, too many questions to know where to start. "Tell me more," was the best I could do.

Junior told me that he had moved down to Bristol last year from Brixton as its yuppification over the last few years had increased rents and other costs beyond his means. As a care assistant for the elderly, a job he'd segued into instead of continuing his medical training after his now late mother suffered dementia, he just hadn't earned enough. His wife, a nurse, had managed to get a well-paid, senior post at a Bristol hospital and his twenty-eight-year-old daughter, Lara, a doctoral student already living in Bristol, had moved in with them to save on expenses and to contribute to theirs. But Junior had failed to find employment despite many applications, not, he thought, because he was black but rather his age being against him.

As a consequence, he had decided to retrain as a psychotherapist (where his age might work for him), something he had thought about doing earlier in his career having always been interested in people and "ow they tick". Temporarily, he was working nights as a security guard on a construction site—as he said, "I may be old but I'm built lacka brick dodo house"—which allowed him the flexibility and time for his course and study.

"Do you want to tell me about the course?" I asked. "You said you're experiencing racism there."

"I think so," he said, leaning forward slightly as if to get a better view of the situation in his mind's eye. "I think it was there right from the start, at the interview."

"In what way?"

"I suspect they wanted a black guy. I'm the only one on the course—one black guy in a group of twenty whites. When

I learned this at the interview, I told them this wasn't good enough."

"And what did they say?"

"They sort of looked a bit sheepish," he replied, holding his huge hands together as if in prayer. "They told me apologetically that the therapy world was dominated by whites and that's why they were so pleased I'd applied."

"Yes, I imagine so," I said.

"I guess it looks good for them to have a black guy on the course."

"That may be true," I agreed tentatively. "I wonder if they might also have been saying they were pleased *for you* that you were challenging this white domination by applying?"

"Yeah, yeah, a token black. Not exactly flooding the market is it?"

It was a surprisingly angry, tangential repost from this gentle giant, and though I very much wanted to get alongside him I was struggling. I wasn't getting his point of view about the racism. So far I hadn't heard anything I would classify in this way with any certainty and I wanted to challenge him. I wanted to ask if there was a diversity of cultures, races, religions, gender identities and sexual orientations represented on the course but I stopped myself, as I imagined what this might sound like coming from a representative of the white-dominated therapy world he was joining. "Was there more at the interview that seemed to you like racism?" I asked, choosing my words carefully so as to neither challenge nor collude with his perspective.

"Someone asked where I'd come from," he said. "I ask you, how racist can you get?" Again I struggled, this time to stop myself thinking of all the innocuous reasons there may have been for asking this question (like being conversationally curious about where he'd travelled from that day). It's not a stance I would normally take: to come up with possibilities in opposition to the ones my client is presenting me with. It's obviously not very useful, especially at such an early stage when getting alongside the client is vital. I was already considering that if we decided to work together after this initial session I would need to explore my own racism in supervision. Maybe I should find a black supervisor. Maybe Junior really needed a black therapist. "And you said …?" I asked.

"Brixton," he chuckled. "I said, born and bred in Brixton."

"You thought they were assuming you weren't Jamaican British?"

"British at all!" he exclaimed. "They thought I was a foreigner!"

"What makes you think that?" I asked, wishing I could say something more empathic like "That sounds awful for you" but instead adding, "Did someone actually say that?"

"Not in so many words," he said. "But I could tell. They didn't need to say it."

I thought about this. Of course, he was right. I'm sure no one would need to have said the words explicitly for him to have picked up on racist undertones. Yet, I remained uncertain. Was it possible that Junior, no doubt the target of racism throughout his life, was over-sensitised to discrimination, so much so that he was hearing racism where it may not exist? I decided to come clean.

"Junior," I began rather hesitantly. "I'm finding this difficult …"

"Yes, sure," he put in. "It's a shock isn't it? Must be difficult for you to hear about discrimination and oppression in your own profession."

"That's not it exactly," I said. "You see, I think in any profession people struggle with discrimination. I think we're all prejudiced to some greater or lesser degree. Everyone has prejudiced attitudes at some time or other because we all fear difference. What I would hope though is that in the psychotherapy world we explore these tendencies and try to understand and transform them …"

"Are you saying you're racist?" he asked, putting me off balance for a moment.

"Er, well," I stumbled. "I hope not intentionally, not consciously—but I have to admit that when we talked on the phone I assumed you were white."

"And you don't like it that I'm black?"

"No, no, my point is that I'd made a racist assumption. I heard your voice and imagined a white man." I explained. "A bit like assuming anyone called a surgeon is going to be a man."

He looked perplexed and I was regretting taking this line. Maybe we were both lost. But then, after a brief hiatus, he said, "That's OK, it's an easy mistake to make. I don't think that's prejudice … just a mistake. I dohn mind." I wasn't sure if he was referring to my racial error, my example of the surgeon, or both. In the event, I simply nodded to avoid further confusion.

In the ensuing silence, what I found most difficult to bracket off was my knowledge of this particular training course that Junior was suggesting was racist. I'd had students from the course as clients and supervisees over several years and, while like any course it had its weaker points, from their accounts I had rather a good impression of it.

Not only that but I'd also supervised a few of the staff, who I'd assessed to be knowledgeable, creative, and, leaning to the political Left, well aware of issues of discrimination and oppression. Indeed, I knew that the course was rooted in the general principle of acknowledging and positively working with difference and had modules specifically dedicated to this very topic.

On the other hand, though from a diverse range of backgrounds and ethnicities, none of these people had been black. Perhaps Junior was picking up an underlying intolerance behind the rhetoric of the mission statement. I recalled the words of an estimable supervisor I'd had in London who'd said, "It doesn't matter if what your client is bringing seems utter nonsense to you. It doesn't matter if you consider their story a total confabulation. It doesn't matter that they've seen fairies at the bottom of the garden or green Martians in the high street. What matters is that you listen and accept that this is their experience."

"You said you wanted to work out how to deal with this racism on the course," I continued unequivocally. "I'm wondering what that might mean and how you think therapy might help you."

Seeming more relaxed now that I was unambiguously referring to racism, Junior explained. He told me how over his years growing up in south London, he'd experienced racism from various quarters: neighbours, doctors (I noted this was another profession he had once hoped to join and I wondered if racism had played its part here in addition to his ailing mother's decline), teachers, the police.

His story brought back memories of my own south London days during the same period; anti-racism marches, banner-waving demonstrations, and some quirky and, in retrospect, questionable Left-wing political movements. But I would not have bumped into Junior in any of these scenarios. He was at home with his head in books or looking after his small daughter or digging his allotment or doing his job visiting the elderly. "Anything for a quiet life," he said, and I detected a note of, what was it, guilt, sadness, resignation, perhaps a yearning for those younger days? I wasn't sure but his demeanour had changed in the telling of his story. He sat bowed and small (for one so large). "What are you feeling?" I asked.

"Oh, maybe I'm a bit nostalgic for Brixton," he said, though his sitting up straight at this point seemed to suggest it was not something he was wanting to reflect on further.

"Tough times back then though I'd have thought," I persisted.

"What? No, well maybe," he said.

"Is there a connection?" I asked. "I mean, between then and what's happening on the course?"

"I guess there is," he replied. "You see, I'm not very assertive. People expect me to be because of my size but I'm no good at confrontation."

"Is that the connection," I enquired. "That you shied away from confrontation in south London when you were younger and you fear you'll do the same on the course; that maybe you'll tolerate anything for a quiet life?"

"Exactly," he confirmed. "I didn't stand up to racists in the past and I need stand up to them now."

Now we had a focus. We mutually agreed we could work together with assertion as our theme.

Over the following months we explored occasions, past and present, where assertion and challenge may have been more appropriate than his default position of compliance; his quietly going along with anything and everything as long as it kept the peace. We also did the archaeology and quickly unearthed the origins of his retiring behaviour within his family—a discovery that came as something of a surprise to Junior, holding as he did an imago of his parents and siblings that was an extremely idealised version of reality. It took some chipping away at, but it was unavoidable that in scrutinising his family and several events within it that his rose-tinted view would eventually become clearer.

His parents had come over from Jamaica in the early 50s, lured by the invitation of employment and the opportunity to contribute to the rebuilding of London's post-war economy in hospital and transport work. His mother, like his wife, trained as a nurse. His father worked as a porter on the railways. Both soon realised that the "opportunity to contribute" was more an opportunity to swell the diminished workforce and to be exploited as cheap labour. They spent the rest of their lives regretting their decision to migrate and continuously hankering after Jamaica (a heavenly place that held magical promises and perfect dreams, though none of the family ever returned there).

The family increased and tightened into its own insular knot—self-referent, self-reinforcing, ostensibly loving, yet totally dependent on a negative "them" to support a positive "us". But even within that tight knot of "us" there were gradations among the beneficiaries, and Junior, the youngest, seemed to gain the least. Though always large-framed and solid, his three older brothers were larger still and kept him in his place by the threat, and sometimes the actuality, of physical brutality.

Not surprising, therefore, that his strategy for survival was one of compliance and non-confrontation, keeping as low a profile as he possibly could. It worked. He survived. Like many an early creative adjustment made to ensure a good-enough existence within families, Junior's strategy got him through to maturity. Unfortunately, as is so often the case, this way of being became his habit and his stumbling block.

Whether his need to keep a low profile led to his academic interests or his innate intelligence just happened to provide convenient cover through his immersion in books and study, I'm not sure—but one thing stood out for me in Junior's descriptions of his family and his place in it: his difference. While his father worked manually on the station platforms and his brothers excelled physically on the football pitch (as well as later in gangs on the Brixton streets), Junior was the "brainy" one, up in the attic, "head in the clouds," as his mother would say, set apart from the rest. Even she, an apparently caring woman at home and at work, was not particularly interested in his academic achievements at school or college, and, turning a blind eye to the more criminal activities of his brothers, showed preference to them. Junior was a bit of a misfit.

"Am I right in thinking that in those days that particular area near Brockwell Park where you lived wasn't a particularly black area?" I asked one session.

"You're right. Our street was mostly white when I was little," he answered. "It's changed now, become more mixed. The yuppies are taking over—black and white yuppies I mean. It's us oldies who can't afford to live there anymore."

"So now age and affluence have become dividing factors," I observed, though, wanting him to stay with his childhood experience, I added. "But back then the big difference for you was being black in a predominantly white area."

"You can't hide the colour of your skin and it wasn't the same as most of the others on the street. The verbal abuse on the way to school was sinting else."

"So at home and out on the streets you were different," I went on. "And as a child and youth you suffered for it in both places. It seems to me you might have struggled to feel you belonged anywhere."

"That's true," he said. "Except around di market ... Electric Avenue, Atlantic Road—places lakka dat yuh wouldn't glimpse a white face at times," he said, sliding into patois perhaps at the memory.

"But mostly, you suffered," I repeated.

"I did," he said gravely.

Junior's fear was that he might keep his head down to get through the course, yet continue to suffer; that he could end up with a qualification in psychotherapy at the expense of being authentic and assertive with others on the course. In our work together we time travelled back and forth between his current experiences and his formative ones and, in doing so, made links between how he was behaving now and the earlier adaptations that he had made and was continuing to enact in current situations. In the useful shorthand jargon, it would be called working between "out there" and "back then". It had some effect in that Junior began to see that the exquisite vigilance he had developed as a child to pre-empt and avoid attacks from his brothers at home and whites on the streets still operated at times—as if the threat of discrimination was still there when sometimes it was not.

"Let's go through this again," I suggested during one session, aware that positives need repeating, re-experiencing and absorbing if they are to affect change. "It seems really important. You said you did an exercise on 'self-image and the body'. You were just about to join two others when a third member cut in."

"That's right," Junior confirmed. "It was like I didn't exist. She just walked in front of me and joined the other two women and I felt totally ignored. And I immediately thought it was because I was the only black guy and they wanted to be a trio of whites."

"And, of course, it was based on many instances from the past where that wasn't just an assumption, that was a fact."

"Sure," he agreed. "But this time I didn't just disappear into the woodwork, I checked it out. I was quite assertive ..."

"I think you can drop the 'quite'," I proposed.

"OK, I was assertive," said Junior smiling broadly. "I challenged what was going on. I was a bit nervous but I put it to them that they'd excluded me on account of my being black. Well, I've told you the rest ..."

"Please tell me again," I implored. "I really want to hear it." This was true but I also wanted Junior to hear his story again too. So he repeated how, in response to his challenge, the women had burst out laughing and immediately huddled around him and hugged him; how he'd been totally nonplussed by their response but found himself laughing too for no apparent reason. It then occurred to him that he'd been excluded, not because he was black but because he was a man and that maybe an exercise on self-image might warrant the women wanting to restrict the trio to women only.

When he put this to them, they laughed even more, telling him he was on the right track, assuring him they could join them and make a foursome, if he felt he fitted the bill.

They asked him to look at them and deduce why they might want to be in a body image group together, what they might be self-conscious of, what they each had in common. "And I looked and I looked," went on Junior. "Then the penny dropped. Big bosoms! They all had enormous breasts! And I hadn't even noticed. That's why they wanted to be together. It was such a relief and it really broke the ice between us—the ice I'd formed myself."

It was a great story and there were others to follow where, in assertively checking out his fears of racism, he discovered more innocuous reasons for his feeling left out or unrecognised. But they were not all light-hearted discoveries of misassumptions. Over time, the group developed enough of a sense of respect and safety to allow for more serious and candid exploration of their prejudices with each other. Their fears of their differing sexes, sexuality, class, education, as well as race, were brought out into the open, faced and challenged. Junior was impressed by the level of honest and authentic disclosure from his peers and began to explore a few of his own fears and prejudices pertaining to assertive women, "feminine" men, and extroverts in general.

It seemed to me that the course was up, running and performing well, and that the work we had done together in therapy had assisted Junior in finding his place in the group. What we had not yet achieved was to bring the work "in here", to explore our relationship and what aspects of his lack of assertion and racism were being played out between us. I realised that, like Junior and the strategy for survival he'd arrived with, I was keeping my head down, not wanting to rock the boat. As he would probably be in therapy with me for the duration of his training, I knew we could not just rest on our laurels for the next three years.

"I notice we haven't addressed what goes on between you and me in this room," I ventured one session. "I even wonder if we haven't both been playing it a bit safe in an 'anything

71

for a quiet life' kind of way. I wonder what we're avoiding?" Junior frowned. I could not tell if this was a sign of puzzlement at something he'd not considered or a sign of defiance at something he did not want to consider, but he remained frozen for several seconds. "You mean about me being black and you being white?" he asked.

"Yes," I replied, relieved he had at last named the elephant in the room from which he had earlier always deflected.

"No problem," said Junior, instantly deflating the existence of an elephant, or at least that it needed addressing. "I've never thought of you as anything but a thoughtful, professional and intelligent man. Your colour is immaterial to me. You could be green for all the difference it would make."

"Really?" I asked, sounding doubtful. "You know, for some reason I don't believe you."

"Now you're just being provocative," he said accusingly but with a broad smile. "You're trying to stir things up a bit."

"I'm not deliberately stirring things up," I insisted. "It just seems odd that we've focused a lot on issues of race and how they've had an impact on you out in the world—but not in here, not here where a white man and a black man are regularly meeting to talk, often intimately, about your life. Could I really be green and you not find that difference relevant to our relationship?"

"You're right, man," he said after a brief ponder. "If you were green, I'd be very worried. In fact, I'd be out the door like a shot! Martians are a very different matter!"

He was laughing, his broad white grin hovered like the Cheshire Cat's before my eyes and I felt a mixture of outrage and fear. *His* difference was getting to me or perhaps it was his *indifference*. Maybe both. Whichever, I had an overwhelming sense of being ridiculed and I didn't like it. "The fact is," I went on, controlling my somewhat wavering voice. "I'm not green, I'm white. You are black. There's a whole historical context of slavery, racism, colonialism, discrimination and oppression between us that we must both carry with us on some level. Isn't that something we need to look at?" His smile disappeared. My anger had not been concealed as well as I had thought.

"Maybe you *are* racist after all to be stressing it so much," he challenged.

"Maybe you're right," I replied. "And, if that's the case, don't you think we should deal with that? Isn't that why you chose a white therapist? Isn't that why you're here? Isn't that why you slip in the patois every now and again—to remind us of our difference?"

For a moment, I thought this outburst of a confrontation had hit the mark. Junior looked like he was deeply impacted by it, considering his response thoughtfully, about to engage with it. I was wrong.

"Listen, Michael," he enunciated in his perfect PR. "You are a well-educated, highly qualified and highly experienced man. I came to you knowing you were white—not because I thought you would be a racist, but quite the opposite. I knew you had the wisdom I needed to explore the racism out there. And you have. Thank you."

"We must finish there," I announced, aware of the time, but also aware the familiar phrase sounded rather final. I think, this time, it contained my doubts about our continuing at all. We had worked well enough. He had got what he came for. So what was it that consistently niggled at me, left me feeling something was not quite right about all this? I watched his large frame disappear through the door as I asked myself, "What am I missing?"

Looking back, it was probably obvious what I was missing. Maybe I just didn't want to see it—so much so that what happened next came like a lightning bolt out of the blue. Even that is an understatement. There's usually a rumble of thunder that gives prior warning and I had ignored whatever rumbles there may have been so the lightning came as an even greater shock.

I had never seen Junior cry but he arrived at our next session distressed and agitated and started sobbing as soon as he sat down in front of me. I must admit that while I felt deeply moved that this giant felt safe enough to be crying in front of me, and wanted to comfort him, I was also relieved that something had broken through his defences. I was even arrogant enough to think it might have something to do with our previous session (maybe that would exonerate me for my outburst). I was wrong again. When he had cried himself to a silent stillness, I asked what he was so distressed about.

"It's hard to tell you," he whispered, his tears welling again.

"OK," I said gently. "You can take your time. I can see it's difficult for you. I can see how upset you're feeling."

"It's, it's Lara ..." he faltered.

"Your daughter Lara?" I asked, imagining something dreadful had happened to her and already feeling sympathy for Junior, whatever it was that had occurred.

"Yes," he managed to continue through his sobbing. "She's got engaged."

I did an instant double take. Engaged? Not ill, not injured or, my worst fear, dead then? Engaged. His nearly thirty-year-old daughter had got engaged. I didn't get it.

"Is that not good news?" I asked tentatively, not knowing how to tread.

"It's the man," was all he said, and for some reason I got to thinking of his age. Maybe the man was very much older. Or was it that he was uneducated? I knew how much education meant to Junior. Then it struck me. "He's white," I stated without so much as a hesitation between thought and words.

"No, no," Junior came back just as directly, correcting my further misassumption. "He's black."

"I don't understand," I confessed, though, maybe a millisecond before he spoke, I think I did.

"Him ah *too* black," blurted Junior. "He's too black!"

The thrownness of life

Since I heard about Anna, I've been thinking a lot about her: about lives and chance, about the arbitrariness of existence. The phrase "an accident of birth" keeps coming into my mind but it's not quite right. More accurately, it's an accident of conception. For Anna, this was the random encounter of a sperm with an egg (the odds against this particular pairing running into zillions) between a sixteen-year-old schizophrenic schoolgirl and a depressed forty-year-old man on a rundown estate in a rundown town where, rumour has it, inbreeding is not uncommon. Not an auspicious start to a life, to be thrown into that particular mix. And the rest of it was nothing to write home about—not that she would have written, as neither of her parents could read, nor were they interested.

Anna, overweight and unkempt, was in her mid-thirties when she came into therapy with me. She appeared for each session in almost the same drab, ill-fitting clothes that even a charity shop would think twice about accepting. She looked so impoverished; the question of how she would pay for her therapy was something we needed to address from the start.

She worked as an office cleaner—she had some savings, she assured me. I told her of my usual fee. She said she knew this and it was affordable for her. I advised her that we might be working together for some time; that I did not do time-limited therapy. I informed her that there were therapists who special-ised in brief-term work, or therapists attached to the NHS who could offer to work with her for free. She had tried all these, she informed me in turn, having been in the mental health sys-tem most of her life. She did not know why, no one had told her, though she did once overhear a psychiatrist describe her as an inadequate personality (the equivalent of describing her as unintelligent when, in reality, she was bright but uneducated).

She was by no means an inadequate person, more a neglected and abused one who found the normal vicissitudes of life too much at times. Her so-called inadequacy, her struggle to cope with everyday social, emotional and intellectual demands, was the almost inevitable result of the inept parenting she'd had due to that accident of conception. Given the circumstances she was thrown into, Anna's adequacy, the fact that she was here and getting by at all, was well in evidence. I thought she was courageous.

In our monetary discussion (more a question and one-word answer session) it became clear to me, if not to Anna, that her wages, even with the savings she'd made from them, would not be enough for ongoing therapy. I offered a reduced fee, pitching it at what I thought was realistically affordable, not patronising to her, not likely to leave me feeling resentful, and on the understanding that if she got more cleaning work or a better-paid job we would reassess the situation. I didn't do this to gain her gratitude (her affectless "fine" might otherwise have disappointed me) but because I wanted her, like her more affluent counterparts, to have the opportunity of therapy.

Anna explained her need of therapy was because she felt isolated and unconfident. She wanted to make friends and find a partner. Her night shift cleaning brought her into contact with very few people, and her days were spent mostly sleep-ing or watching television in her flat. Anxious in any situation involving other people (supermarket self-checkouts were a boon for her), she went about her life silently and alone.

Of course, I could not guarantee that she would find friends or partners to end her isolation but I considered that helping her to become more confident through our therapeutic work together was feasible, and that potentially this could lead to the achievement of her other desires. What that work would be took me some weeks of recalibration to discover.

I question whether it was therapy as most people would understand it. But I think, I hope, it was therapeutic. I suspect most people would say we just chatted (and they'd be right)— about her week, her work, her meals, her TV viewing, anything and everything we could think of (though initially it was I who initiated the topics) in order to hold a conversation— something she had not previously experienced.

To begin with, I found our attempts at conversation, the halting staccato of our exchanges, uncomfortable. Teaching someone to converse (surely something that evolves quite naturally throughout childhood) is not something I've been trained to do. I flew by the seat of my pants a lot of the time but gradually relaxed into it once I realised the only way to improve conversational skills is to keep on having conversations. In the early days they went something like:

"So you had fish and chips for supper."

"Yes."

"What fish did you have?"

"Cod."

"Was it good?"

"Yes."

"Is that your favourite fish?"

"Yes."

But, within the first year, we made advances. Anna learned that conversation is a two-way thing; that details can be provided without having to be asked, and that it's all about curiosity—about being interested and interesting. I'm not talking scintillating conversation here, but it was much improved.

"I had fish and chips for supper," she would say (it was only later that we addressed her dreadful diet). "And I really enjoyed it. I love eating cod and chips, don't you?"

"I do occasionally," I would reply.

"As long as the batter's crispy," she would say. "I hate soggy batter!"

"Me too! There's nothing worse is there?"

"Well, there probably is …"

"Like?"

"Well, I think tripe and onions is disgusting. What's your worst food?"

She could not remember ever having a conversation with her parents about anything. When we eventually got around to exploring the past, probably in the second year of our conversations, her memories of life at home were mostly of her mother upstairs in bed (either medicated to oblivion or manically talking to herself) and her father drinking himself into a stupor in front of the television day and night. The infrequent times they walked down the road to the social club they would sit in silence at a corner table, nursing their beers. No one spoke to them, or they to each other.

It was the same at school where she had no friends and spent most of her time hiding away, trying to avoid contact with anyone. Teased and bullied in the classroom and playground (the teachers seeming oblivious to this) it was no wonder the art of conversation, that basic necessity for relationship and a sense of belonging, eluded her.

By the end of year two of our strange work together, Anna was exchanging niceties at staffed supermarket checkouts, chatting with people on buses, and talking to complete strangers walking down the street. The latter necessitated work on the appropriateness of some of these encounters: her naive enthusiasm needed reining in at times in terms of the people she was talking to and the subjects she was choosing.

She lacked, so far, any sense of the needs of others and of what their motivations might be. Now she'd found her voice, she'd swung indiscriminately from one end of the distrust/trust spectrum to the other and expected anyone and everyone to be keen to engage with her. I was concerned she might get hurt or exploited in her childlike innocence.

It was at this time that I came to understand the full extent of her naivety. In one of our chatty conversations she disclosed her sexual abuse by her father. Not that she called it that. It was her father's "special thing" he did when mother had "mad episodes" and was taken away to the mental hospital for weeks at a time.

I was appalled to hear of this trauma (another among so many), and I noticed she referred to "our" bed several times in the telling. I wasn't sure what she meant but, gently exploring further, it transpired that there was but one bed in the house until she was thirteen years of age. For those many childhood years she had slept between her naked parents who had snuggled and stroked her "all over" night after night and had sex with each other with her in their midst. She thought this was normal. She thought this was what all children experienced. She had no one to say otherwise. And, if they were aware of the abnormality of this behaviour at all, her parents would have known she would tell no one as she talked to no one anyway.

It was only in recent years that she had realised she must have become pregnant due to her father's performing his "special thing" in her mother's absence and that this was why she had been allowed her own bed in her own room at last. Ignorant of anything to do with sex and menstruation at the time, she had thought her miscarriage to be simply a heavy bout of the monthly pain and bleeding she had begun to experience.

The more I learned of Anna's early life, the more my admiration grew. I have worked with many clients who have experienced trauma in one form or another in their lives but Anna's was of a different order: Anna's was multiple, extreme, continuous, and pervasive. It was physical, sexual, emotional and psychological abuse without respite. Her only saving grace was that she had little understanding of the aberrancy of what was happening to her: a small saving but enough to keep her surviving. But although on many levels she did not understand—did not even know that what was happening to her should not have been happening to her, her body knew. It grew protective layers to shield her from others and it flooded her with anxiety and panic attacks to keep her isolated and, consequently, "safe".

It was incredible that someone who had known no love, no compassion and no caring from anyone in the world throughout her life; who had been misused, abused, bullied, ostracised and neglected, even into adulthood, had enough inner strength left to keep going. I often thought, had this been me, I would have given up. What I was most aware of, and struggled at times to find a therapeutic use for, was my rage—my fury at what life had randomly thrown her into and subjected her to. Where were the good-enough parents, the interested neighbours, the attentive teachers, the safe social workers, the thoughtful psychiatrists? Where, in all this shit of a life, was someone who cared? I thought *I* did.

In the third year of our work together, at her instigation, Anna slightly increased her payments to me. She had found several people who were only too glad to take her on as a cleaner in their private houses, and were happy to pay her more than the contract firm she worked for ever did. By this time, her attention to her clothing, her choice of a more stylish and varying attire, made her more presentable and employable.

These were not things we ever addressed directly. They happened incrementally as her confidence in herself increased. And along with that increase in confidence, she began to socialise, more discriminatingly, beyond the occasional conversation in the street. She joined a slimming club (though the slimming part of this was somewhat lost initially, as she and several others frequented the chip shop next door straight after the meeting) and she got to know a few people there, eventually well enough to suggest meeting up for walks and cinema trips. And this brought us to the topic of transport and travel.

Anna's journey to and from her therapy involved a bus, a local train, and a substantial walk along the canal towpath. Often anxious on her journey, she knew she could always get off the bus or train at the next stop in surroundings familiar enough for her to get home. This knowledge helped her manage her anxiety enough to continue on this circuitous route that took her almost three times longer than the session itself. So tenacious was her dedication to attending therapy that she hardly missed a session, whatever the weather, and when on the few occasions she felt an imminent panic attack when about to walk across the aqueduct at Avoncliff she would phone me from her mobile and ask me simply to talk to her and encourage her across the bridge. Eventually, resisting looking down over the parapet, she could calm herself by hearing my voice in her head and had no need of phoning.

This journey was the longest she had made in her life. Her parents had never taken her beyond the perimeter of the town they inhabited, so this was quite an achievement. She had exceeded their circumscribed travels but any further distance for her seemed impossible. Attempting it (as she bravely did) she would feel so anxious she would have to turn and make for home as quickly as she could. So far, she had not seen this as too much of a problem as she could easily keep her life restricted to the local environs, but when her newfound friends wanted to go on outings further afield, she felt frustrated at not being able to join them.

"I want to go with them to Bristol," she told me, enunciating "Bristol" in such a way it sounded the most exotic of places. "I can't do it. I feel frightened just at the thought of going so far."

"What is it that you feel frightened of mostly?" I asked.

"Being out of control, lost in a strange place, panicking, not being able to turn around and get back home," she replied eloquently and without hesitation. "If I'm walking, I'm in control. I know where I am. Even over the aqueduct, I know I can always turn and walk back—but I can't turn the Bristol InterCity train around."

"But a car you could," I found myself saying without any consideration. I expected Anna to respond to this idea with scornful dismissal. Apart from the leap of confidence she would need, the expense would be prohibitive. But she was up and running with it. "A car, of course," she said, beaming at the thought. "I'd be in control. I could go as far as I wanted. I could turn around when I chose. I could stop and get out. I wouldn't be at anyone's mercy at all."

"No," I agreed. "You would be at no one's mercy. You'd be in control. You'd be able to say enough is enough."

The practicalities were not as problematic as I'd imagined. Her alcoholic and perpetually recumbent father had a perpetually recumbent Fiat parked on the forecourt of their flat. It had remained unused since he'd lost his job some years ago. Prior to that it had only been driven from one side of town to the other, and together with the fact that it was "acquired" almost new it had very low mileage. Her father made no objection to Anna's taking possession. He didn't really have the energy or interest to care.

Anna took on some extra cleaning work and booked her driving lessons. Despite her anxiety and the occasional feeling of panic (more in relation to being confined in a car with a somewhat gruff driving instructor than to learning to drive) Anna passed her test first time. The feeling of freedom and expansion it gave her was reflected in her very being. She now drove to her sessions (a much shorter route by road) and would arrive jangling her car keys with obvious pride. It was a time of great excitement as week by week and little by little (sometimes only a few yards) she drove further out of her home town, down country lanes she hadn't known existed, to villages beyond my home, into Bath, even out the other side of Bath. Her goal— Bristol. She was going to make it. I was certain.

This must have been in about the fourth year of working together, and, as she ventured further out into the world, over the months we revisited her past—her childhood and her abuse. We took stock of how, despite the hand that life had dealt her (and which she now knew was an exceptionally terrible one), she had come through and achieved so much. As I write this, I realise how meagre it all may seem: she had learned to hold a conversation, gained a few friends, had more lucrative cleaning jobs, took better care of herself, and drove a car—things most people have or do without effort; without any sense that they are things to which they are anything but entitled. But Anna had no sense of entitlement, and not much of an idea about possibilities. These changes and achievements were for her the equivalent of a severely physically injured person learning to walk again—or more than that—learning to run.

The cough Anna developed around this time sounded dry and made her voice sound slightly hoarse. There was an epidemic of coughs and colds that early spring and it seemed that Anna had fallen victim to it like several other of my clients, family, and friends. I felt fortunate not to have caught it myself as one after the other my clients cancelled sessions, feeling too unwell to even contemplate a phone session. Anna stalwartly made it to each of her sessions but, as the others' health returned and they resumed their therapy, it was evident that Anna was not recovering. If anything, her voice was sounding even more throaty and she told me (I nearly wrote "complained" but that would be far from Anna's tendency) that sometimes she found it difficult to swallow, experiencing it as if there was something, a swelling perhaps, partially obstructing her airway.

Inviting though it was to explore the possible psychological and emotional connections to her physical symptoms, the epidemic and Anna's sorry state led me to think I might be adding insult to injury. Rather, I insisted she get herself checked out by her doctor, who, ascertaining that Anna had few symptoms remaining that might be cold-related, sent her to the local ENT department to see what was happening in her throat. Nothing, it appeared.

The diagnosis was globus hystericus, a term with which I was unfamiliar but could hazard a guess as to its meaning. Sure enough, my research suggested that the sensation is probably brought on by emotional stress, which may cause tension in the muscles used for swallowing, rather than anything physical (like an actual lump). It seemed I could have explored Anna's emotional/psychological state more usefully than sending her off for check-ups. But at least we knew now what to be looking at. "I wonder if you've been feeling more anxious than usual in these recent months," I floated by her, following the diagnosis.

"I don't think so," she replied in the deeper voice I was getting used to. "No more than I ever do."

"Nothing about what we're doing that might be feeling a bit stressful?" I asked.

"You mean chatting?" she said, her slight smile indicating this was a joke and needing no response from me. "Or it might be Bristol," she added quickly, perhaps a little unnerved by her own jesting.

I made sure she saw I was smiling in appreciation. "It could be too much of a stretch, you mean?"

"Right now, maybe—but it's my goal," she said, adding imploringly. "I want to get there."

"I know you do," I assured her. "But how about leaving it for now, how about taking a few weeks off from pushing yourself? You've reached Saltford and that's an enormous step."

"Saltford is still Bath really," she replied dejectedly. "It's definitely not Bristol."

"It's getting there!" I said, trying to cheer her up, as she looked so crestfallen. "Listen, let's wait until the better weather. Take some time to relax, get your throat better, and enjoy what you've achieved."

"OK, but only for a few weeks," she agreed reluctantly.

Despite pushing herself less and resting more, as the weeks went by Anna's throat worsened. She was also getting short of breath. Concerned that this was more than a psychosomatic stress reaction, I suggested she visit her GP again. Following further tests, x-rays and scans, an updated diagnosis was made. Anna had a rare form of lung cancer. Of course she did. It was terminal. Of course it was. This was Anna. This was the woman who all her life, from that miserable moment of conception, had been dealt crap by the hand of fate. Inevitably, it was not simply going to be the awful-sounding but innocuous globus hystericus. How could it be? Anna's life could not allow for something so banal and inoffensive. Terminal lung cancer it had to be.

I realise how deterministic I sound, as if it was decreed all along that Anna's life would be a dreadful one. This is my anger speaking: my rage at the unfairness that Anna had suffered so much and that now more suffering was being piled on thick and fast. I'm struggling with language here. Again, "unfairness" implies causality, as if something or someone is being selectively unfair—is doing the piling on. In a calmer mood, I recognise the thrownness of life is just that: random, without cause. It just is.

Anna was far more matter-of-fact about her diagnosis. At least, so she appeared. I was not sure she'd fully grasped the actuality that she was fatally ill even though she told me she'd been given only a couple of years to live. It may have been that she was still desensitised enough (though less so through our work) by all that had happened to her in her life not to feel the full impact of her situation. She didn't cry. She didn't rage. She seemed to accept that her life would not be a long one; that her hope of finding a partner was not to be fulfilled, as if this was simply the way of things. She underwent her first round of chemotherapy as if it was just a bit of an inconvenience, while I was pondering our future together.

I knew, without doubt, I would work with her to the end of her life. I determined that even if she could not pay, I would continue to see her every week. I also decided at that time that if her health began to deteriorate I would drive her to Bristol—better still, I would help *her* to drive to Bristol. As her passenger, I would talk her to her goal in the same way I'd talked her across the aqueduct.

In the meantime, Anna showed little sign of deteriorating. Just the opposite. Whilst most people would have succumbed to the sickening effects of toxic drugs being pumped into their bodies over a period of several weeks and taken to their beds or, at least, to resting, Anna seemed to thrive on the chemotherapy. She continued to do her cleaning jobs, attended the slimming class (though neither the class nor the cancer was making any difference whatsoever to her size), went to the cinema with her newfound friends, and, most importantly for her, continued to drive a little bit further each week. She was determined to surprise her friends one day by driving them to Bristol. By Easter, she had managed to drive to the first Keynsham roundabout, and there was not much between that and the big city. It really looked like she would get there under her own steam after all.

After her third round of chemotherapy, the tumour in her lung had reduced by two-thirds its original size. Anna had been given the results, and a better prognosis, a few weeks before our summer break. She was ecstatic. We both were. "I'm so delighted!" I exclaimed on hearing the news.

"Me too!" she declared, her voice almost back to normal. "*And* my consultant! He thinks it's a bit of a miracle."

I held back from saying it was about time miracles happened for her, as I realised I might be advocating a religious perspective to which neither she nor I subscribed. Even saying she deserved something positive happening for her would, in effect, be reverting to determinism. But I wanted to somehow acknowledge this turn of events. More, I wanted to acknowledge her.

"I think you're amazing," I blurted out, warmly and spontaneously. She looked startled and a bit uncomfortable and I noticed she'd coloured a little down the sides of her neck.

"Me?" she said, in all genuine modesty. "Do you really mean that?"

"I really do," I said, in all genuine honesty. "I think you are truly amazing."

"You'll be even more amazed after the summer break," she predicted.

"Oh, why's that?" I asked, though I had a suspicion what she'd say.

"During your holiday, I'm going to make it to Bristol," she stated emphatically.

But she didn't make it to Bristol. Nor did I see her again. When she failed to turn up for her session in September I was concerned. Not badly, just anxious that perhaps she'd forgotten which week we were restarting. I left a message on her mobile to say I was sorry not to see her and that I looked forward to seeing her the following week. When again she failed to turn up I really was concerned, anxious that her cancer may have taken hold again. I left another message on her mobile and I wrote her a letter to her home address, being as discreet as possible in case she was in hospital and her parents might be opening her letters and getting someone to read them.

87

But it was not her parents who contacted me. It was one of her slimming club friends who, in place of Anna's useless parents, had kindly taken on the role of her executor and come across my letter some weeks later. Anna was dead, she informed me. It was not the cancer. She had been killed at a crossroads when an HGV had failed to stop at the lights and crashed into the side of her car. I did not ask if she had been injured or had died instantly. I did not ask how long ago this was or how her friend was feeling. I asked immediately where it had happened. And when I learnt the crash had occurred in Bristlington, my very first thought was that maybe that counted, maybe a suburb of the city counted. But I could hear Anna's voice loud and clear in my ear saying "No, it's definitely not Bristol", and I sobbed.

So, I've been thinking a lot about Anna since I heard: thinking about the thrownness of life and the irony of her "accident of conception" coming full circle in her accident of death. I think of her with love and great admiration. I think of her and her dreadful life angrily and sadly, but most of all regretfully. I regret that I had waited, that my timing was so badly wrong, that I didn't care enough. In the knowledge gleaned so early in our work together that bad things happen to Anna, I should have travelled literally that extra mile with her; I should have got her to Bristol.

Armadillo

It had snowed for three days and dense, heavy flakes continued to fall. The valley was so white it was hard to distinguish tree from field except occasionally when the dark, moving speck of a distant cow helped make out one from the other. It was a beautiful sight but my delight in it was tinged with concern. The access to my house, and therefore my consulting room, down the steep lane from the village was nigh on impossible. Most of my clients had made it for their sessions in the previous two days by parking at the top and walking tentatively down the final stretch, but by Wednesday morning the previous snow had turned to ice and walking up or down the lane was treacherous.

My first client of the day was happy to be offered a telephone session. The next preferred a video call. Both had phoned earlier, having checked the local roads, to discuss these arrangements and had kept their usual times. But I hadn't yet heard from Chris, my eleven o'clock client, as I waited near the phone a few minutes before the hour, anticipating that he would call from his home some thirty miles away.

On the dot of eleven the doorbell rang, and Daisy, usually a reliable forewarner of visitors, began barking. Even she hadn't ventured out all morning: I was surprised that anyone had.

Shushing the dog, I went to the door to be met by a peculiar sight.

Chris, who I would normally describe as "heavily built", stood before me, snow-covered and almost twice his normal size. Not only was he dressed in several layers of coats and scarves, he wore a huge fur-trapper's hat with ear flaps that reached right under his chin, making his already bearded face look twice as wide. But it wasn't just the hat that caught my attention. The strange, dilapidated contraptions strapped to his feet were just as compelling. I can only describe them as wooden racquets strapped together, and to his hiking boots, by a tangled arrangement of twisted string. I pulled the door open wider to allow him the necessary extra room to pass into the porch, and invited him to come up when he was ready. "Ok, mate. It might take me a while," he said. "Especially the snowshoes."

"Ah, that's what they are," I thought to myself.

Quite why I was so surprised Chris had made it for his session I don't know. If anyone was going to make it, it was Chris. He was confident, bold and domineering and had all the makings of what one might refer to as "a man's man". In fact, with his passion for following soccer, playing snooker, drinking real ale (sometimes to violent excess), and tinkering with his car at weekends, not to mention his patronising attitude to women, he proved the stereotype. So why not add driving through snowstorms on hazardous roads to the list? Of course he'd made it. He was duty-bound to prove his credentials as a "bit of a lad" though he was well into his mid-forties.

There was, however, despite his intrepid front, one area in which Chris's credence had become threatened. He was currently sexually impotent. If it weren't for this, as he'd made clear several times in the few sessions we'd had so far, he wouldn't be "touching therapy with a bargepole" (a metaphor whose irony I kept to myself). Recently, after nearly three decades of promiscuous, mostly drunken one-night stands,

Chris had simultaneously met someone special and lost his erectile power. To put it another way, his one-night stands had flopped.

Before long, I heard his heavy tread on the stairs. True to form, he was taking them two at a time and was soon in the room. Now reduced to his former but still ample size, he sat down with legs wide apart, arms folded across his chest, and with a look of satisfied accomplishment on his face. I just knew I was meant to comment on his achievement. Anyone else and I might well have done, but with Chris I was reluctant. I didn't want to encourage his constant need to prove himself. He sat awaiting some words of approval and I sat and waited for him to speak.

"Bit slippery on the side roads," he eventually pronounced in his "you-know-how-it-is" monotone. "But the main ones were gritted and the M4 was a doddle. I can't understand why people chicken out just because of a bit of snow."

I sat and said nothing, though the words "common sense" had crossed my mind.

"People can't handle the challenge," he continued. "My old man would have been out there come hell or high water. He never missed a day on the beat. Wouldn't have let a bit of snow get in his way. The absenteeism these days … People don't know they're born."

"I noticed you've mentioned 'people' three times," I observed, failing to control my slightly irritated tone. "Who are these people?"

"Oh, everyone," he replied with a loud exhalation as if to blow them away but too bored to do so.

"That must include me," I suggested, attempting to narrow the focus from the whole world to us in the room.

"You?" he questioned. "Well, no, obviously I don't mean everyone."

"Maybe you do," I persisted. "And maybe you do mean me. After all, you've been driving in dangerous conditions while

91

I've been sitting here safe and warm. I wonder if you see me as unable to rise to the challenge."

In slightly changing his words, it was my turn to have used an ambiguous turn of phrase. I pondered whether he might be seeing me in a competitive light, needing me to be impotent like him or, more likely, more impotent than him. "So I sit here warm and relaxed while you risk the elements," I went on, noticing the increased tension in Chris's posture and the tightening of his arms across his broad chest. "You rose to the challenge while I waited passively for you to come." Whether or not Chris explicitly heard the double entendre, his body seemed implicitly to respond to it as he quickly clenched his knees together and braced his arms around him even tighter. I felt like I was facing an armadillo, its vulnerable underside protectively hidden beneath its thick leathery plates.

"Well, mate, I wasn't expecting you to come and get me!" he exclaimed with a forced chuckle.

"No?" I responded provocatively, not quite knowing why but feeling it had something to do with piercing armour.

"What!" he exclaimed startled, for the first time unfolding his arms and holding them out as if reaching for something. "You'd never do that!"

I noticed he'd made me the subject of the action. I noted too that he'd quickly folded his arms again. "Probably not—but would you never want me to?" I asked, returning the initiative to him.

"I don't understand," he said, and I could tell from his furrowed brow that he didn't, at least not cognitively. But his body, squirming slightly, seemed again to register some other form of understanding. "Well, I'm just exploring," I said quietly, not wanting to scare him away. "I wonder how often in times of need you reach out to people, to your girlfriend for instance."

"To Maria?" he asked. "She can't drive a dodgem! I don't think women were made to drive." Fleetingly, I contemplated challenging this sexist remark but then Chris would have

92

succeeded in diverting from the theme. I was more annoyed that, with my own prior deflection away from our relationship, I'd missed an opportunity. Was I, too, feeling uncomfortable staying with what was going on between us? Was I, like Chris, avoiding intimacy—rescuing him, and me, by moving the focus outside the room? Whatever, having mentioned his girlfriend I decided to stick with it. "I wasn't so much thinking of driving," I continued. "I was more thinking of how in the weeks we've worked together I've only heard about how you look after Maria, how you generously give so much to her— your time, your attention, your money, your ..."

"Oh mate, she deserves it," interrupted Chris. "She's so attractive and funny and intelligent and ..."

"She sounds lovely," I interrupted in turn. "And you want to give her so much—but there's one part of yourself that you're not yet able to give."

"Yes," he said emphatically and then fell silent a while. "She says it doesn't matter," he eventually added without much conviction.

"Not yet," I said.

"No, not yet," said Chris. He seemed both sad and scared as he looked at me for a split second before dropping his gaze to the floor, and I thought how even an armadillo might betray its feelings in its unprotected eyes.

"What are you feeling?" I asked.

"Nothing," he replied too quickly.

"I thought I saw some emotion in your eyes."

"No," said Chris shifting uneasily on the sofa. "Look this is a waste of time. I told my GP I just needed Viagra."

"Ah, your default position," I put in accusingly.

"What?"

"It's just that in almost every session whenever you get near to feeling something you mention Viagra."

Chris grunted.

"What were you feeling just now?" I persisted.

Chris closed his eyes as if to better remember, and sighed a long, slow sigh as if to calm himself. Then came the first soft-underbelly thing I'd heard him say, "I'm scared I'm going to lose her."

"Yes, of course," I said empathically, hoping he'd stay with that feeling.

"But why?" he asked, more angrily than imploringly, avoiding staying with his scare by favouring his need for understanding. "Why is this happening?"

"I wonder what's different," I threw in.

"Different?" he repeated with a slightly baffled inflection. "I don't know ... everything."

"What's everything?"

"Oh, you know, everything. I just want to be with her," he explained. "She's the only woman I've ever felt like this about."

"Felt like ...?" I probed.

"Oh, I don't know, mate, in love, I suppose," he offered reluctantly, "love" probably being a word relegated to use only by women, children, and lesser men. "Is that the problem?" he asked. There was such a plaintive note in his voice as he said this that I felt an unexpected warmth towards him. I knew how excruciatingly difficult this was for him; not only to be here talking about himself to another man in this way, but hearing himself express things he'd probably not allowed himself even to think.

"I think maybe it is," I concurred. "As an adult, I think she's the first woman you've ever loved and needed. You don't usually let yourself need anyone so I can imagine how anxious you might be feeling." This was too much. I'd misgauged his level of tolerance and, even as I spoke, I knew I'd made a mistake. I should have let him find his own way to answering his question. Instead, I'd attempted to lead rather than track my seemingly tough but deeply sensitive client. My summary, with its weighty additions, was far too emotive. In my eagerness to capitalise on the connections he was making, I'd blown it. Chris drew his armour plates around him and talked for the rest of the session about his impending snooker match and his previous successes at the club. I tried to bring us back to his feelings but he was having none of it. I resolved to learn from my mistake and be more sensitive to his pace and level of tolerance.

Sometimes, however, it's the after session—the off-guard moments between therapist and client—that has a more profound effect than what transpires in the prescribed fifty minutes. While I sat reflecting on the session, half aware of Chris down in the porch, huffing and puffing as he struggled to put on his layers of clothing, he shouted up, "Hi mate, can you help me please?" I knew it wasn't a *cri de coeur* concerning therapeutic possibility but, even so, I felt touched by his request and went down to him. The reassembled yeti pointed to the snowshoes onto which he'd stepped, explaining that he should have strapped them on before he'd put on his several layers as he bent forward to prove there was no way he could reach his feet.

Without hesitation I knelt down and did the best I could with the tangled strings. Embarrassed, Chris stood silently, shifting his weight from side to side, reminding me of a child having his shoelaces tied and wishing he could do it himself. But he couldn't. He'd needed me to do it, and he'd asked. "Cheers mate," he said heartily as I got to my feet, slapping me on the shoulder manfully before trudging off, equally manfully, into the white landscape.

Over the ensuing weeks, in more clement weather, we continued our meetings. Viagra reared its head (so to speak) whenever we got near to his emotions, as did soccer, snooker and anything else not threatening to his constructed masculinity. For this reason, I suspect, he avoided mention of sex and his current inability to achieve an erection (for him, the epitome of masculine failure).

For a different reason, I avoided it too. I held the view that though sex was proving a problem for Chris, sex itself was not the problem but more a symptom of his psychological and emotional state. I'd expressed my opinion on this from the start but Chris wasn't getting it. At least, not until several weeks after the deep snow session, at a time when I'd been encouraging him to talk about his mother—a subject almost as much avoided as sex, and clearly not unconnected. "I thought of her the other day," said Chris, whose voice I'd noticed becoming less monotone in recent weeks.

"Oh yes?" I replied, hoping I didn't sound too pleased to have successfully brought his mother into the arena.

"The day I came wearing those snowshoes …" he continued. "D'you remember?"

"I do remember," I assured him (how could I forget those strange contraptions and the tangled strings?) "What made you think of your mother?"

"The fact that she wouldn't have done that."

"Helped put your shoes on?" I enquired.

"That too," he answered enigmatically, and then seemed to struggle with further revelation, his mouth opening but no words ensuing. I moved slightly forward, perhaps only a few centimetres; not too much to scare an armadillo, but enough to look into his saddened eyes and show I was there wanting to hear.

"She wouldn't … she wouldn't even have come downstairs," he managed to stutter. "In fact, I wouldn't have asked her to help. There'd be no point asking, 'cos she never did. So when I asked you and you came downstairs and tied my shoes without a second thought, I thought of her."

It was true. At the time, I hadn't given it a second thought. In the circumstances, it had simply felt right. Only later did I hear my old supervisor's voice saying, "Gratification is an avoidance of grieving". I knew what she'd meant but I'd questioned it by asking her, "Always?" and, looking me straight in the eye over the top of her spectacles, she'd simply nodded. We'd argued about it and eventually agreed to differ.

Much as I could see that there may be times when fulfilling a client's desires—to be loved, to be held, to be special—might merely paper over the cracks of the original loss or lack (bypassing the unexpressed grief that needs an outlet), I also believed that sometimes, as now with Chris, the deficit and the grief may surface by being met. He was sobbing profusely and I encouraged him to stay with his sadness without talking for a while, and sat quietly watching as his tears trickled through his straggly beard.

The story Chris eventually told was not unfamiliar. It could be summed up in a long list of clichés—don't be so soft, don't be a baby, don't blubber, don't bother me, and many more such prohibitions. More succinctly, "Boys don't" could simply be added to a whole range of ordinary human behaviours, a list that came mostly from the mouth of Chris's domineering mother but which was also modelled exquisitely by his father, a retired policemen, and two older brothers, one in the army, the other a professional boxer. But it was more than the modelling and verbal admonishments Chris had received in response to any expression of needs or feelings that had necessitated the growth of his armadillo's armour. It was clear from the story of his early years that he had not been responded to physically (apart from violently) by any of his family.

I pictured him as a baby, his sensitive skin crying out for contact, wanting merely to be gently touched and safely held, or as a hurt toddler running for comfort to someone's unavailable arms. I imagined the gradual submission of his body to its isolation within itself, those plates developing over his soft, raw skin like successive layers of resin hardening. In subsequent sessions, some layers seemed to melt as he allowed himself to express the anger and sadness he'd stored for so long.

I have to admit I'd hoped this catharsis might free up his libido; that his sex drive would be swept along with the forceful wave of his emotions. But Chris needed another accompaniment to that expression to fully release his libido. Sometimes insight, a precursor to choice, is invaluable in creating a more holistic connection, especially for someone like Chris, who'd repressed and protected his feelings beneath a cognitive and physical shield.

"I can see how I came to be like I am but I still don't understand," admitted Chris after several weeks of grieving the lack of a mother who would answer his simple need to be himself. "My brothers don't seem to have my problem."

"As far as you know," I added.

"As far as I know," Chris echoed. "I don't suppose they'd talk about it."

"No," I said. "Not the done thing in your family to talk about such things, especially about impotence." Chris writhed in response to the final word. "But siblings' experiences are rarely the same and, in any case, wouldn't necessarily have the same outcome," I continued, intentionally distracting him from his discomfort, at this point more involved with the sense he was making of everything. "I'm not concerned with them. I'm only interested in you." Chris seemed to take this in as he responded with a simple but acknowledging "Yes".

"You said you didn't understand," I went on. "But I have a hunch you're beginning to make some connections between your past and what's happening now. Am I right?"

"I don't think so," he said. "What makes you think I do?"

"Well, in recent weeks, you haven't mentioned Viagra," I replied. "Maybe that's a sign."

"That's true," he agreed with a smile of recognition. "But I'm still not getting the connections. I still don't understand. I want to—but I'm finding it hard to put it all together."

"Let's take a different tack," I suggested, appreciating Chris's willingness and honesty. "A while back, you said you were 'in love' with Maria."

"So?" said Chris somewhat belligerently. It was clearly not yet a phrase he could sit with easily.

"Well, I was wondering about the other women in your life before Maria," I said. "What was different in your relationships with them?"

"They weren't," he answered immediately. "I mean they weren't really relationships. I didn't know them that well at all. Sometimes I didn't even get to know their names."

"They were just women to have sex with," I suggested.

"Yes, they were real dolls, just a bit of fun," he said with a laugh. "Men have needs you know!"

"And these women answered that particular need," I said. "You needed sex and you got it. But with Maria ..."

"I need so much more," put in Chris, the penny seeming to have dropped.

"Not just an object to get your rocks off with—fun though that was?"

"Cor blimey, guvnor," said Chris in a mock Cockney accent. "You got me bang to rights you 'ave!" And he laughed. Though I was mindful of the possibility of us joking away what I'd said, I laughed too. Keeping our eye contact, it felt like a meaningful moment between us as we laughed together. It seemed to me that Chris had really got it. His eyes were shining. He sat relaxed. Far from his former habitually defensive posture, he now seemed open and vulnerable.

"Will you say some more?" I requested. Having learnt from my previous mistake, I wanted to respect his pace and avoid imposing my own ideas on him. He sat scratching his beard for a while as if deep in thought. I imagined the firing of pathways in his brain, connecting the deep felt sense of those bodily "knowings" with words that could organise and express them.

"It's like, when I'm with Maria, it means too much," he explained after a while. "It didn't mean anything with the others. It was just physical, 'getting my rocks off' as you put it."

"Like with a doll," I suggested, hoping he could see how his earlier reference to the reality of dolls meant just the opposite.

"Exactly," he confirmed. "Could have been inflatables! But with Maria, I want her so much. I'm not sure how I can put that, except it's everything. It's physical and mental and emotional and everything else too."

"Everything else like …?"

"I'm not good at this," he faltered.

"I think you are," I contradicted. "You just have so many voices saying you shouldn't be."

He smiled. "It's like a fucking football crowd inside my head!"

"Ignore them," I suggested. "I doubt they're on your side."

"What, Swindon Town?" he quipped.

"Second division?" came my repost.

"Yeah, yeah, we'll get there," he laughed.

"So will you," I said, aware of the 'light-relief' diversion and wanting to bring him back. "You were talking about more than 'scoring'."

He looked contemplative again, remaining silent for a few moments.

"I think it's to do with being so close with Maria," he said.

"Would 'intimate' be the word?" I suggested.

"Yes, intimate, that's exactly it," he answered, seeming pleased with the word. "It's bringing up all my intimate needs from the past. Like when ages ago you said about coming to get me and I said I knew you never would. I didn't know it then but I think I was talking about my mother. And like when you put my snowshoes on, that was intimate too, wasn't it? And it made me think of my mother again."

I wanted to say something, to congratulate him on his perceptive connections (so much better expressed than mine would ever have been) but again, remembering how pushing him had closed him down, I held my tongue to avoid intrusion.

"But I'm not thinking of having sex with my mother when I'm wanting sex with Maria!" he protested vehemently, and I thought it expedient to add a gentle "No". Such a thought was clearly repugnant to him, and though there was conceivably some unconscious, convoluted truth to it, I couldn't see it being helpful at this point.

"So what is it?" he asked himself plaintively. "My mother's in it somewhere—the hard-nosed bitch! Do this, don't do that!

Be this, don't be that! What about me? What about my needs?" He fell silent, and though silence is sometimes golden, in this instance it felt more like a grey cloud of defeat. "I guess sex is like expressing a need," I put in, hoping to add a glimmer of light.

"It sure is!" responded Chris. "But now it's become too risky. With Maria it's more than sex. It didn't matter with the others. Whether they were up for it, or said 'Get lost', it didn't bother me. It was sex that was being rejected, not me."

"So with Maria you risk being rejected as a person?" I asked rhetorically.

"Yes, a person with needs, lots of different needs," he elaborated. "Like with my mother!" he then exclaimed. "I knew she was in it somewhere!" To his relief, Chris realised it was not a sexual association with his mother that was inhibiting him but an intimate one—one that didn't happen for him as a child with his mother—and one which he now feared would not happen with Maria.

It meant risking a repeat of his early failure with his unresponsive mother. Getting close risked, at best, rejection, and at worst, abandonment—something Chris had voiced some weeks previously in his fear of losing Maria. At that time I'd referred to the wonderful attention he gave to her. Now, astutely, Chris realised that what he had been giving to her was what he himself longed for. It was there. It was on offer. But he kept these possibilities at bay by his scrupulous, one-way care of Maria. An early formed part of him dare not risk accepting her nourishment, even allowing it, in case it disappeared again.

"What do you need from Maria?" I asked.

"I need her to just hold me," he replied, wrapping his arms about himself, not defensively but soothingly.

"So ask her," I said.

The following week brought with it summer storms and torrential rain. The hills on the far side of the valley were shrouded in a murky mist and not even the distant speck of a cow could be seen. My first two Wednesday clients, undeterred by the incessant downpour, had arrived drenched and, despite their umbrellas, in need of towels to dry their dripping hair. I was looking forward to seeing what Chris might be wearing against such conditions, and imagined him in an oilskin jacket and sou'wester—most likely in bright yellow. But, unusually, in fact uniquely, for Chris, he did not arrive on the hour. Maybe the flooded roads were delaying him more than the snow had managed to do.

It was only after five minutes had past that I thought to check my answerphone. Sure enough there was a message. It opened with a cheery "Hello, Michael"—in itself a refreshing change from the ubiquitous "mate" of former times—and continued with an explanation of the terrible road conditions and poor visibility. No doubt his dad would have made it, but Chris was not even going to try. He was staying at home with Maria and would see me next week at the usual time. He made no request for a telephone session and I thought it best not to return his call.

With fifty minutes to add to my lunch break I decided to make a treat of this unexpected expanse of time and just relax. I made myself a cup of tea, settled down in my favourite chair, and opened the newspaper at the cryptic crossword. Usually, starting on a blank grid can be painfully slow for me. I have to chunter over several clues before my logical mind is able to melt into more lateral thinking. With Chris still occupying my thoughts it wouldn't have been surprising had I struggled even more to make a start, but when I saw the first clue— *Musical postulant, confused with toy mannequin, unearths New World digger* (9 *letters*)—both Chris's dilemma and the crossword answer were beautifully elucidated. I had a feeling that Chris had found a solution too, though one very different to the crossword.

Seven deadly sins

I wake myself up screaming "No!" and lie there trembling for some minutes trying to remember what I've been dreaming about. But dreams need to be exited slowly and gently if their convoluted meanderings are to be transmitted from unconscious imagination to a conscious mind seeking sense. My sudden awakening erases all trace of what has been going on in my fantasy world, leaving only a sense of having been through something challenging. Whatever it was that had led to my frightened and imploring scream is not forthcoming despite my attempts to insert possibilities—hooded attackers, stampeding monsters, devastating news—into the void.

It's not a good start to a busy day, and the feelings of dread and frustration remain with me as I dress quickly, breakfast on the hoof, and read through my emails, most of which I condemn to the trash without the usual satisfaction I get from hearing the scrunching sound as they disappear. Even walking through the woods with my dog in the bright morning sunlight does not manage to alleviate my disturbed state as it normally might. I just have to hope I can bracket off this sense of unease well enough to work with my clients.

Luckily my first session of the day, an initial interview with a prospective client, distracts me immediately. Lolita's opening gambit is to tell me I look older in the flesh than on my website. Nothing better to take my mind off things than to be told I've aged since the photo was taken (only six months ago) but, actually, she is right. My recent diet may have helped me lose over a stone but not entirely where I'd intended: my stomach has shrunk only slightly whilst my face has shed copious amounts of fatty deposits it can ill afford to lose, leaving me looking somewhat gaunt. Still, I feel healthier being lighter and reassure myself of this fact before giving a slight nod to acknowledge what Lolita has observed and ask her if this is significant to her.

"Oh yes it is," she answers. "Very much so. You see I'm looking for a therapist more my own age." I look at her more closely in the ensuing silence, checking on my first impressions. They remain unchanged. I may not be a particularly accurate assessor of age but despite the youthful years suggested by her black leather miniskirt (already riding up beyond mid-thigh) and pink FCUK T-shirt (the black lettering spanning both her sagging breasts), unlike her fictional namesake, this Lolita is anything but young. In fact, I think Nabokov would have shared my assumption based on the rest of her appearance—white hair, wrinkled face, gnarled and liver-spotted hands, painfully thin wrists—that she has at least a decade on me. Even then, I think I'm being kind to place her in her seventies.

"And you are how old?" I ask, sounding as nonchalant as I can.

"I'm thirty-two," she replies, straightening out her wrinkled stockings that I've already marked down in my mind as surgical. Satisfied with her hosiery, she looks me straight in the eye. It feels like a challenge.

"Oh, in that case I am very much your senior," I announce. "What a pity this means we won't be working together."

"Well," she says, elongating this single word in what I imagine is meant to be a salaciously teasing manner. "Maybe age isn't everything. You know, you're still quite attractive for your age."

"Could this therapist be a woman?" I ask quickly in a desperate bid to deflect her from further attempts at seduction. "I know several excellent female therapists around your age."

"I'm not into women," she announces. "Tried it, of course, but lesbianism doesn't quite do it for me, you know? It's pleasant but not so satisfying as with a man."

"Really?" I say, not really meaning to encourage her, but it does.

"Oh, yes, I'm sure you feel the same about women," she goes on. "I mean, it's the difference that counts. You know, if you and I were naked together, well, you'd be captivated by my female genitalia, I'm sure. You wouldn't want me to have a cock now would you?"

I stay schtum. The very thought of her displaying any genitals, male or female, induces my hurriedly eaten breakfast to regurgitate. I swallow back a horridly acidic gob of something I'd rather not identify.

"You look a bit green," says Lolita, and I seize the opportunity.

"Actually, I'm not feeing at all well," I answer pathetically. "I'm sorry but I'll have to end our interview. Maybe I could send a list of younger therapists for you to try?"

"Male," she asserts (as if I could have forgotten). "But I'll have a think. You know, you might suit me. I've been feeling horny all through the session so you must be giving me the right signals."

Waiting for Sloan, my next client, I check my address book for any young therapists I may know but, feeling guilty at the thought of foisting the deranged Lolita onto any of them, I wonder if perhaps a referral to the mental health team might be more appropriate. This would, however, need discussing with her and I dread another meeting. I decide to postpone the decision, realising I've spent quite some time pondering on it and that Sloan is now over twenty minutes late. His email greets me as I open up my mail:

hi M—overslept—missed job intervu—not keen anyway—2 much like hard work—staying in bed—gr8 place—might C U next wk if can bother—:) S

I am never quite sure with Sloan whether he's illiterate, very literate in text-speak, or just too plain lazy to write complete words. I suspect the latter, as it tends to be his modus operandi (he would say MO) in everything else in his life. I think he's managed to attend a quarter of his sessions, and then be late for those.

But Greg is here on time. He's never late—not because he particularly appreciates our sessions, but having paid for them (with his private insurance) he wants his money's worth. No doubt, on this strangely disturbed and disturbing day, he will be the first client to have a whole session. He sits in yet another new designer suit, hands behind his head, one foot on the knee of his other leg in what I can only imagine is meant to be a relaxed but powerful pose, staring at the ceiling. I feel, as I often do with Greg, underdressed, even scruffy, by comparison. I rather like the feeling. I wait.

"Michael, I was thinking about something you said last week," says Greg, not changing his posture at all, still staring at the ceiling.

"Oh yes?" I reply, surprised.

"You asked if having so many simultaneous affairs might indicate something lacking in my marriage."

"I did," I say, remembering my confrontation full well. "And you've been thinking about this during the week?"

"No, it only came back to me just now," he replies, dashing any hope that he might have really reflected on something. "I just wanted to tell you you're wrong."

"Ah," I sigh. It's a disappointed sigh. "I wonder how you see the situation then. I mean, you have an extremely beautiful wife and yet several other lovers. In fact, I've lost count of how many. Currently?"

"Seven," Greg says without hesitation. "All very special women—amazing in fact."

"A bit like your houses," I suggest.

"What?" he exclaims. "Like my houses? I don't get you."

"Well, I'm aware you have several 'amazing' houses dotted around the country …"

"The world," he puts in.

"Indeed, but why do you need so many?" I ask directly.

"I don't need them," he replies. "But why not—if I can have them?"

"That's what I mean," I say.

"What?" he sounds genuinely puzzled.

"Well, you say I'm wrong to suggest that a lack in your marriage might be the reason for so many other lovers—so I wonder if it's more that the same applies to women as to houses. Why not—if you can have them?"

"Oh, I see, yeah," says Greg, seeming pleased with the insight, and for the first time lowering his upturned, now smiling face to mine. "You're right. Why not if I can have them? Why not have more of a good thing?"

"I just wonder if there's such a thing as 'enough' in your world?" I ask, wanting to wipe the supercilious smile from his face. "Women, houses, suits …"

I hesitate. This is meant to be therapy. It's more like an interrogation. What am I doing attacking him like this? Surely, I should be non-judgementally attempting to understand this young man—this very wealthy, smart, half-my-age young man. But I can't stop myself.

"… Cars, holidays, swimming pools, yachts. Is there no end to your accumulation of possessions?" I spit out the final word with contempt. Greg, however, seems oblivious to my envious attack (not that I'm envious of the possessions. I'd just like to experience what it's like not to have to think about the utility bills). He changes posture at last, puts both feet on the floor and brings his arms to rest at his side, a quizzical look on his face.

"What are you thinking?" I ask after several moments have passed.

"I'm thinking about your question 'Is there ever enough?'. It's a good one. It's a very good question," he says. "Quite a challenging one."

I am pleased that my outburst, though perhaps not something I'd like to admit to in supervision, has penetrated his Armani suit. "And do you have an answer?" I enquire, now quite gently.

"Never!" he instantly shouts. "There's never enough. I want more and more. Why not? As you say, if I can have it, why not? You've really helped me to see that really clearly today. I feel you've given me permission to simply go and get what I want. What's that saying, 'more is more' or something like that?"

"Um, not quite," I manage to insert feebly. "Less is ..."

"More therapy too," he interrupts. "I want it three times a week at least."

I feel relieved the session is over but continue to dwell on my envy of Greg's wealth and my verbal assault on him as I make for the kitchen. For some reason, despite my earlier queasiness and lack of hunger, I feel an urgent need to eat. I open my dilapidated fridge thinking of Greg's most likely American, two door, almost walk-in (no, probably fully walk-in) larder-fridge in his mansion's designer kitchen, the one in Bath or London, Paris or LA—it doesn't really matter.

I stuff a chicken leg in my mouth as I hear the expensive fart of his Maserati speeding away. The chicken sticks dryly in my gullet. I spy some leftover sausages lurking behind something bluey-green and unrecognisable and I demolish them ravenously as if I haven't eaten since they were cooked four days ago. I could make a healthy salad and use a knife and fork but I feel such an urgency to fill my stomach—there's no time for such niceties. The phrase "why not if I can have them?" spins around in my head as I plunder the bottom shelf for hidden fodder.

Inexplicably, I crave cow pie and rootle around the bottom shelf in the firm belief that such a thing exists, and exists in my fridge. The chorizo ring makes a poor substitute and I need to wash it down with a carton of orange juice that tastes more like grapefruit juice being well beyond its "best before" date. "Best before vomiting" is the thought that passes through my mind seconds before heaving up in the sink. But it isn't this thought that induces what might have been a self-fulfilling prophecy; it is rather the image of Lolita that has just flashed before my eyes as I note the resemblance of the chicken skin to her wrinkled surgical stockings.

Somehow my lunch hour flashes by in a trice and, clueless as to how I recovered from my biliousness and made it from my kitchen to my consulting room, here I am sitting with Priddy (a name she invented after visiting a village of that name in Somerset at the age of three, feeling even at that age that Gertrude was demeaning and highly unsuitable—she refused to answer to such a misnomer and her family soon succumbed to her demand).

As I sit waiting for her to begin, I recall our last week's session at the end of which she had said she was thinking of finishing therapy with me. She'd heard of a brilliant psychotherapist who had recently moved into the area with credentials on his website that knocked mine into a cocked hat. I did not enquire what they were but she had managed to mention before leaving that his clients included royalty and celebrities. I'd wondered if he advertised this on his website and whether I should add "works with ordinary people" to mine.

Priddy clears her throat and looks at me directly with her piercing blue eyes. "I've decided to continue in therapy with you," she announces somberly, as if pronouncing her own death sentence.

"OK," I reply non-committally. "I'm interested to hear how you came to that decision since I saw you last."

"I simply decided he wasn't suitable," she says, omitting to provide any reason. I comment on her reluctance. She is unforthcoming.

I ponder aloud, "I wonder if it has solely to do with him or me. I have a feeling someone else is involved." This is not an intuitive supposition on my part—more my knowledge of Priddy's tendencies. There usually *is* someone else involved in one way or another somewhere along the line in Priddy's decision-making. Her psychological survival depends upon others with whom she can compare herself, compete, and proudly emerge as the better of the two. I have a suspicion something has gone amiss in her quest for supremacy.

"Actually, it's that ghastly woman from Number 12," she admits, apparently finding no difficulty in being so predictable. "You know, the one who thinks she owns the street—walks her dog up and down every day wearing garish slacks and high heels." (I assume she means the woman rather than the dog.) "Never thinks to use a poop bag and I've never seen her in Waitrose."

I am baffled by the non sequitur and wait for the denouement that I'm sure will come eventually. In the event, I fathom it very quickly.

"I bumped into her the other day," she continues, disbelief redolent in her tone.

"In Waitrose," I suggest, thus providing the connection.

"Yes, in Waitrose of all places. Irene Baker in Waitrose!" Her eyes have begun to dart apoplectically as if searching out Irene, her trolley no doubt stacked higher than Priddy's, somewhere along the sacred aisles of Waitrose.

"And the relevance to your decision is …?"

"I'm coming to that," she responds sharply. "That awful woman caught me at the checkout. I hoped none of my close acquaintances were there to witness it—heaven knows what they would have thought! Anyway, she started talking about her nerves and I was about to tell her about the free CBT she could get on the NHS when she announced, loud enough for everyone to hear mind you, that she'd found an amazing therapist ..."

"Who works with royalty and celebrities," I put in, aware I was completing her sentence for the second time, mostly to stop myself nodding off.

"Exactly!" she exclaims.

"And this led you to change your mind?" I enquire. "The fact that your neighbour is in therapy with this amazing therapist."

"That's just the point. Don't you see?" she asks rhetorically. "If he's working with Irene Baker, he can't be amazing. He can only be a fraud!"

Of course, this quirky logic is completely understandable within Priddy's frame of reference in which she defines herself by her desire to be more important, special and attractive than anyone else in her environs. But as my role is to challenge her fixed perception of the world and her place in it, I feel beholden to confront her.

"It could be that he's a very good therapist," I suggest. "Especially working with someone who has a nervous complaint."

"Nervous!" Priddy explodes. "That woman has the audacity to parade around the neighbourhood wearing fluorescent pink. She talks to all and sundry—donkeys and hind legs come to mind. I can hear her raucous laugh from my kitchen. No, she's not at all nervous."

"I don't doubt her apparent confidence," I continue as calmly as I can. "But by 'nerves', I suspect she meant something along the lines of chronic anxiety, which might be why she appears to grate on you so much. Perhaps this therapist is a specialist in anxiety disorders."

"I doubt that very much and she's not royalty," asserts Priddy, clearly not keen on my attempt to normalise either Irene or the therapist. "And she's certainly no celebrity."

"Neither are you," I remark unhesitatingly, in an attempt to force a reality check in amongst all this grandiosity.

"I'll have you know I've traced my ancestry back to Queen Boudicca," she claims and, not content with just one startling piece of self-deception, informs me that her third cousin once removed starred in a crowd scene in *Far From the Madding Crowd* (which I suppose, at a stretch, could be referred to as a title role).

"The point is …" I begin but realise I haven't the faintest idea what the point is. I've totally lost the plot. I'm falling down some vortex that's spinning crowns and supermarket trolleys and sheep about me as I plunge into the depths.

"Anyway," says a voice from somewhere outside the cortical flow. "I managed to put Irene in her place when I told her about you. She seemed quite put out when I informed her you're familiar with Bowie."

All I can hear as I hurtle downwards, packets of Waitrose Duchy Originals whirling around and past me at a rate of knots, is my disembodied voice shouting "Bowlby, woman, it's Bowlby!"

I am now with Ray. I have no idea how I escaped from the vortex nor do I remember Priddy leaving and Ray arriving. Somehow, one has morphed into the other quite seamlessly. I don't think I've moved an inch. I cross my arms to test whether I'm able to make any sort of movement and find, to my relief, I still have control of my body.

"That's a very defensive posture," remarks Ray: ex actor turned executive coach with little distinction between the two as far as I can see. It's never occurred to me before but I find myself thinking I could refer Priddy to him—an executive coach might be much more to her liking than a lowly psychotherapist and, having trod the boards, he could well count as a celebrity.

Should I tell him why I've folded my arms? Should I tell him that it is indeed a defensive position in preparation for the rage I'm predicting will be forthcoming at any moment? I unfold my arms and say nothing.

"If there's one thing that makes me so mad," says Ray, true to form and apparently not that interested in my body posture after all. "It's being interrupted."

I take care not to say anything, though I am wondering whether he's referring to conversational, sexual, eliminatory or just any general sort of interruption.

"Right in the middle of my lecture on 'The importance of timing in executive coaching' a blasted mobile starts ringing," he continues, failing to see the irony, his voice already rising a decibel or two and his face reddening like a quickly ripening fruit. "Well, I won't have it! And I let this arrogant youth know it. I told him to get the hell out of my lecture room and never darken it again." Ray's voice has taken on a deep, melodramatic timbre that along with the increasing volume creates a vibration through the floorboards. At least I think that's what's happening, or maybe it's me trembling—praying I haven't inadvertently left my mobile in my pocket—as he bellows more about the folly of youth, the lack of rigour in the education system, the sorry state of the roads in Bristol, throwing in something about obesity for good measure, though whether any of this applies directly to the young man in question I have no idea. I wait for a pause in his tirade.

"It reminds me of the time your father ..." I begin.

"My father! My useless father!" shouts Ray, shaking with anger at the very mention of the man. "Don't you dare bring my father into this room!"

"I think he's already here," I dare to say, suddenly feeling braver in the face of the bullying rage that Ray directs at

113

everyone and everything at every opportunity. "Angry dad, angry son—chip off the old block I very much think."

For a moment I wonder if I have really just said that. Ray's response confirms that I have. "You keep your thoughts to yourself if they're the best you can do!" he booms across at me. "You're bloody useless! You're meant to be helping me deal with my insomnia and all I'm getting is verbal abuse."

"Maybe your father's in both of us. He's very much here now in all this anger" is what I think I'm saying, in a very warm and empathic way, but what I hear coming out of my mouth, loudly, clearly and aggressively, is "You couldn't coach a frigging flea to jump." Where has that come from? Why am I saying it? Could it be some useful enactment we're getting into or is it yet another sign that I'm losing the plot? Ray seems not to have noticed. He's talking about hating everyone who wears blue. I'm wearing blue. Should I change? Do I mean my shirt? Or do I mean my therapeutic stance? He's off again … "It makes my blood boil the way birds fly. I hate the bloody things with their flappy wings. Why can't they walk like everyone else? Bloody outrageous! Who do they think they are …?"

The doorbell rings downstairs. Ray continues oblivious to the interruption. I can't imagine who it can be. Thankfully, on this ridiculous day, Ray is my last client. It might be just a neighbour calling by. I ignore the bell a few more times while Ray is demolishing the health care system and anyone who likes Schoenberg, but the bell keeps ringing and I feel I have to answer it. I stand and make to leave, telling Ray someone is at the door. Furiously, he grasps my arm to prevent me leaving and lectures me about interruptions, which apparently make him so mad but I feel already I know this. "This is where I came in," I say as I leave the room.

The doorbell is now ringing uninterrupted as if someone is standing holding it with continuous and urgent pressure. I race down the stairs in response and throw open the door. It is not a pretty sight. Lolita, one hand on her hip, the other on my doorbell, is stark naked but for a thong that she's clearly had difficulty putting on, and a purple feather boa, like a chain of seabirds drowned in an oil slick, hanging round her neck down to her bare feet. Her fungally infected toenails, painted bright green, provide no relief from this visual onslaught.

"Hi Michael," she shrieks over the noise of the bell, her crimson lips pouting. "I've been horny all day just thinking of you, so I've decided you must be the right guy for me. I thought we could start with a therapy session right now ..." And with that, she throws her arms tightly around me. With her face now but seconds away from mine, she extends her yellow snake-like tongue towards my mouth.

I wake myself up screaming "No!" and lie there trembling for some minutes trying to remember what I've been dreaming about. But dreams need to be exited slowly and gently if their convoluted meanderings are to be transmitted from unconscious imagination to a conscious mind seeking sense. My sudden awakening erases all trace of what has been going on in my fantasy world, leaving only a sense of having been through something challenging ...

Let's face it

Whe I first meet with a client I don't charge a fee. I know it's still my working time but I see this initial session akin to someone buying a house, or clothes for that matter: the potential customer having a look around the house, or trying on suits, before deciding if it's quite right for them. I encourage prospective clients to shop around to find a therapist with whom they feel comfortable and yet challenged enough to form a good enough "fit". After all, it's a working relationship that, like a house or a suit, may need to be lived in for several years. But following this advice could be an expensive business if several therapists are being visited and require payment for an initial interview, so I feel I'm doing my bit to alleviate the expense by this no-fee policy.

The analogy weakens when I look at it the other way around, referring as I am to a mutual assessment. I too like to have the freedom to judge whether working together might be feasible and I'm not sure a house-seller or shop assistant has the same freedom to turn away customers. But I want the facility to decline to work with a client, and I think I'd feel uncomfortable taking their money and rejecting them at the same time. So my motivation is a mixture of my own selfish comfort and my concern for the client, though I have no idea what the ratio of comfort to concern might be. As it is, I have rarely declined to work with anyone.

The few who spring to mind include a self-described neo-fascist member of the National Front (you can see from the movement's name how long ago that was, me being quite a novice therapist at that time and probably scared of him), a young anorexic woman who was so weak and emaciated I thought she would be better served by a specialist in eating disorders, and an extremely negative and belligerent middle-aged man who threatened that if I didn't "cure" his depression in six months he would kill himself (terms with which I was unwilling to agree). There are not many others, but nonetheless I maintain my stance—just in case.

This first meeting is unpredictable for both parties involved. There's a lot of hope, fantasy, assumption and anxiety felt before we've even met. When these are brought into the room and we are in each other's presence, I want us both to feel, as far as we can, that our exploration towards deciding to work together or not is based on our experience of each other as human beings as well as in our respective roles. In other words, on our mutuality as "fellow travellers" into unknown territory as well as our sense of the potential in our asymmetric relationship of therapist and client.

Fine words, I hear myself say, as I think of my recent encounter with Charles to whom it seemed initially that the very concepts of "fellow" or "relationship" were anathema. I remember my chilly discomfort when he phoned asking to speak to "Doctor" Martin and his obvious disdain when I corrected him. Plain "Mr." clearly didn't fulfil his expectations of a professional. He was one of very few clients to interrogate me about my qualifications. Not that I have any objections to such enquiry but I could tell from his throaty growls down the phone that he hadn't a clue what they meant, despite my patient explanations. What he did seem satisfied with eventually were words like registered and accredited (by whom or to what didn't appear to matter).

When I asked him what he was hoping for in seeing a psychotherapist he immediately turned the tables, and more belligerently than authentically, I suspect, asked me what a psychotherapist did anyway, in response to which I suggested we could meet to find out what he was wanting and what I could offer. I informed him that I did not charge for this initial exploration. This was the first and only thing in our conversation that seemed to please him, as he had seen several others who had charged "outrageous amounts".

I spent a few minutes reflecting on Charles after his call. I had an image of a tall yet stocky man; perhaps because I thought his resonant, bellowing voice (somehow even the occasional throatiness of it resonated) needed an echo chamber large enough to produce such amplification.

My fantasy was of a public school-educated, landed-gentry background and a man who had benefited from wealth that had diminished in his lifetime. I saw him suited in brown, probably with leather patches at the elbows, definitely with a tie, bald headed, and sporting a moustache but not a beard. I imagined him to be in his early 70s, retired. From what? Banking? Running a country estate? I struggled to place him. But I had him married in a loveless (right from the start) marriage with several children and grandchildren.

I got the impression he wouldn't know an emotion if it hit him in the face (a phrase I was to learn only later to be so poignant) but that inside somewhere was a deeply hurt man. But what he wanted from therapy and what, if anything, I could do for him was, as yet, a mystery. I recognised I was both curious and anxious to meet him but doubted we would decide to work together.

When I opened the door to the tall and stocky Charles on the dot of his appointed time I found it difficult to contain an involuntarily intake of breath. I disguised it with a slight clearing of my throat as I held out my hand to shake the wizened one he held out to me. I shook it with care, it looked so painful. It was gnarled and so twisted out of shape it was more like a claw. I was struck by how dry it felt.

But it was his face I stared at, glanced away, stared back, not knowing which was the right thing to do: both feeling inappropriate, unnatural, and unkind. Yet I could not just look at him "normally". This was outside my normal experience. I wanted him to help me, to provide me with some guidance, to tell me to look, not to look, how to look, where to look. But he did not. His face (webbed down one side with what? Scars? Ridges? Thickened skin?) remained impassive as I directed him to my consulting room. I would have followed directly but I remained at the bottom of the stairs breathing deeply, gathering myself before joining him.

I noticed as I sat down that he had carefully positioned himself at an angle on the sofa, presenting to me the undamaged side of his face. I registered for the first time that he was younger than I'd anticipated but, as in my fantasy, he was bald (though he sported no moustache and I wondered if he would have done so had his scars not prohibited it). He was dressed as I had dressed him in my prior rumination but that was the last of any accuracy in my prognostication about him, as I was about to learn. I opened with my usual gambit, "So what brings you here?"

"Bad start," he replied in a voice even more booming in person than on the phone. I wondered if his injury affected his hearing, at least on one side, as such volume was not at all warranted by our close proximity. "Stupid question," he went on. "Just ask me what my symptoms are and be done with it. I know you're not a doctor but at least you could act like one."

"Would you feel less uncomfortable if I *was* a doctor?" I asked, ignoring his bullying as best I could, determined to make it clear that I was not a doctor, and that I would not be acting like one.

"What?" Charles spluttered.

"I was wondering if talking to a medic might be more comfortable, more familiar to you than talking to a psychotherapist," I replied. Then, tempted though I was to avoid reference to the obvious, I took the plunge, "I imagine you've had a lot to do with the medical profession because of your hand and face." For a moment Charles looked startled but pulled himself together almost immediately and stated flatly, "Yes, well, that's true."

As he spoke, he turned his face to me full on. It felt like a defiant rebuke for my having had the audacity to draw attention to it. It was also the first time we had made eye contact fully; the connection seemed adversarial, but at least it was a connection. I found myself already thinking there might be a glimmer of potential in us working together, but what I had hoped was a pregnant pause between us soon became a barren stare-out that, after only a few seconds, I chose to break.

It did not feel appropriate to be playing a game of chicken at this early juncture, and wanting to avoid a long stand-off I glanced away and then back. "So perhaps coming to see someone who works mostly with feelings and inner processes is a bit more difficult for you than seeing someone who deals mostly with the physical," I suggested.

"Do you think for one minute my years of medical treatment were easy?" he snarled with a snarl that looked the fiercer for being unilateral. I felt the urge to point out that I had carefully not implied this in anything I had said and that I was talking of comparative discomfort, not easiness, but I suspected this would make no difference.

"I'm sure none of it was easy," I said instead. "Do you want to tell me about it?"

"There's nothing to tell," he replied curtly. "That's not why I'm here."

"OK," I said. "What brings you here?" We had come full circle but perhaps something had shifted during our brief, tense exchanges. Perhaps I had passed some test that Charles had set me unconsciously. He seemed not to notice the repetition and responded without his original defensiveness.

"This is difficult," he said almost inaudibly. "I'm not used to talking about myself. I think I learnt very early on how not to do that. I ... well, I might as well say it ... I think I'm homosexual. There you are. I've said it." I looked at him expectantly, waiting for more but nothing was forthcoming. "And?" I asked.

"What?" he asked in return, sounding surprised.

"You think you're homosexual and that brings you here because ...?"

"Because I'm sexually attracted to men!" said Charles, raising his voice but not quite to its former volume.

"Yes, I understand you're telling me you might be gay," I explained. "What I'm not yet understanding is why that has brought you to therapy." I wasn't being deliberately obtuse. I've worked with many people, admittedly much younger men and women, struggling with their sexuality but somehow such a struggle seemed incongruent with the man who sat before me. Somehow I didn't buy it. But Charles was determined to sell it.

"Why? For Christ's sake man!" Now he exceeded his former volume. "I'm fifty-six-years-old. I'm disfigured. I live an almost reclusive life as an artist ... happily and successfully, I might add. I've never had a friendship, let alone a relationship in my life. I don't need them. And now I think I might be gay and have to contend with that! That's the problem. That's why I'm here!"

"And his name is?" I asked point blank.

"What?" He spat out that word yet again. The complete "What the hell are you talking about man?" remained unspoken but was clearly communicated through the spittle-sprayed ending of the single word.

"You've just described your life as a recluse," I explained to him. "For fifty-six years—that's such a long time—you've managed to hide yourself away, doing your art, avoiding people, not needing them, detached from everyone it seems—all apparently happily and successfully. So why would it matter if you were straight or gay or sexually attracted to geometric shapes—unless you'd met someone who'd disturbed that carefully constructed independent life of yours?"

"Ah," sighed Charles. "Well, I haven't met a triangle." I smiled, relieved that he had a sense of humour (another indication that we might be able to work together), and asked my question again. "His name is Chris," replied Charles with obvious affection.

Though it took me many questions before I managed to piece together some sort of narrative, I learnt that Chris was a talented picture framer who Charles had approached professionally some years ago when he had had a large exhibition of his work in Bath. Their meeting was out of necessity rather than choice, as were his dealings with galleries, art material suppliers, the postwoman, the village shopkeeper, and so on.

It became apparent that Charles' life was more peopled than many others' might be; peopled rather than personed. These were contractual arrangements, not subjective relationships. Charles liked it that way and, obedient to his preference, they dealt with him in a totally business-like manner: efficiently, expediently, clinically, no fuss, no niceties, no real contact. I surmised that this avoidance of personal connection made "facing" them more tolerable. But Chris, apparently undeterred by Charles' brusque and repellant manner, had entered his life and, over time, pierced his defences.

Chris had insisted on being a person with him, and through his lively and attractive personality induced Charles to relate to him as a person too. He had even persuaded Charles to disclose details of the terrible accident in childhood that had caused his disfigurement—details I was not to learn of at all in our meeting. Such intimacy would need trust and time.

"And Chris is gay?" I asked, wanting to understand just how much of a problem this really might be, thinking that if Chris was straight it could be a big one, and that Charles' attraction for the unavailable might be at the heart of the matter. But it turned out that Chris was definitely gay and out and proud and liked by everyone, and unattached and only slightly younger than Charles.

"So what's the problem?" I asked gently.

"You still can't see it can you?" snapped Charles, back to his attacking posture. "You think this is all very plain and simple don't you?"

"I don't think I see it that way," I replied carefully. "But what you may be picking up is that I'm not understanding what it is that is disturbing you so much. There's something more than your attraction for Chris and I'm not sure what it is."

There was a long silence in which I observed Charles as he looked out of the window to the valley. I found myself drawn to his scars, the wizened skin, the puckered ridges that ran from ear to eye, and the mottled blues, reds and yellows that subtly coloured his cheek like a moth's powdered wing. I saw a handsome man. I saw something beautiful in his face despite, or maybe because of, his injury. How quickly my initial revulsion had transformed.

It was not hard to imagine Chris, nor anyone for that matter, being attracted to the man who sat before me. Apart from, that is, his unattractive manner—the bullying personality he had developed to keep people at bay. It was more this than his face that made him grotesque and repellant. This was his deterrent. But Chris had not only seen through it but broken through it. Chris had got to the heart of him.

"It's not my attraction for Chris that's the problem," said Charles, breaking the silence, then pausing as if wrestling with himself to speak more. "It's the fact that he doesn't know of my attraction that is so difficult. Being around him, enjoying him, maybe even loving him is exquisitely painful. I just want to know how to deal with it. That's really why I'm here."

"So you're attracted to Chris but he doesn't know?" I reflected back to him. Charles nodded, confirming that I'd grasped the situation. But I wanted to understand it completely, and I didn't. "He doesn't know that you're attracted to him because you haven't told him or shown him … (Charles nodded) … and you haven't done either because …?"

"He mustn't know," asserted Charles. "I couldn't bear it if he knew."

"You couldn't bear it if he knew you were fond of him," I stated, and in the repetition finally thought I understood. "Because if he knew, he would have to respond in one way or another. He would have to accept or reject you."

"The latter—that's the only way it could be," he said categorically. "Let's face it, why would he be attracted to me? Why wouldn't he reject me?"

"'Let's *face* it?" I put in, quickly pouncing on the elephant that had re-entered the room. "You're afraid that he'll not be attracted to you; that he couldn't be attracted to you, because of your face?"

"I wasn't ready earlier," said Charles defensively, as if I'd challenged his former denial that his appearance was why he was here. "It needed a context."

"Yes, I understand," I assured him and we both paused a while. It was an important point to have attained and I really did understand his need to have reached it in his own way. I took it not just that the context of the story had been necessary for his eventual revelation, but that he had needed time for us to create a context between us in which he could feel safe enough to face himself with me. I watched and waited.

"Bit of a mess, isn't it?" he said, staring at his gnarled hand as if intending a double meaning. "Not what I'd expected at my time of life! Unrequited love is ..."

"It's not unrequited love," I interrupted. "It's unde-clared love. But you fear it may be unrequited if you were to declare it."

"It's not *maybe*. I *know* it." he said, contradicting me in turn.

"You *believe* it," I said. "For all you *know*, it could just as easily be the opposite."

"Well," he said with a throaty edge of distaste. "I think you're just being Pollyannaish!"

"I don't think so," I asserted. "The context you've described seems a positive one to me."

"I don't understand," he replied, obviously nonplussed and more than a little irritated. "A positive one? I've just told you I'm in agony."

"Well," I began, now not absolutely certain what I'd meant but certainly feeling it, and now feeling for words to express it. "The context as I understand it is that for the first time in your adult life you've let someone stir your inner world. You've managed thus far to keep everyone else at a safe emotional distance—you've not had to face them, nor really had to face yourself. But one person has appeared who is challenging your status quo by his very presence."

I paused and looked across at Charles. His eyes were moist but he managed a smile that I took to be recognition before I went on.

"Now, I don't expect for one minute that there have not been others, men *and* women, who would have liked to get closer to you. But you haven't let them. You've kept them away from you by your bullying tactics. You've kept them merely as utilitarian objects in your life. So I ask myself, why is Chris the exception? I doubt he's the only attractive person you've ever met but you've not allowed them to stir you, you've stuck to your reclusive script with them. So my hypothesis is that Chris is the exception because on some level you can sense he is very much attracted to you, and that this realisation is very painful because it goes against all your carefully crafted beliefs about yourself."

"Pure psychobabble!" snapped Charles, his moist eyes now dry.

"Sure it is," I agreed instantly. "Except I wonder why you're responding to it so vehemently if there's not at least a grain of truth in it?"

As I said this I detested that, without meaning to, I was executing that somewhat stereotyped psychoanalytic manoeuvre of trapping the client: either the client agrees with the therapist's "correct" interpretation or in protesting too much against it still "proves" the therapist is correct. I was wondering how best I might extricate Charles from this double bind when he saved me the trouble. "So if there's any truth in all this nonsense," he inserted. "What are you trying to say— that I'm stubbornly refusing to let my life be better? That my fear of being rejected isn't real? It all feels very real to me."

"I know it all feels real," I said gently. "I can see how very painful all this is for you."

"But?" he put in angrily.

"But," I obliged. "Though your fear of rejection is, I'm sure, very real, I have a sense that acceptance might equally be frightening for you. And by withholding your feelings from Chris, in effect, by rejecting him, you risk neither. You simply stay with the pain of not knowing."

We remained in silence for a while. I wondered what was going on for Charles as he sat impassively staring at his with-ered hand. I was aware that neither his hand nor his face had figured much for me for most of the session. I similarly imag-ined it did not figure much, if at all, for Chris. I reflected, as our initial interview was drawing to an end, what a strange session it had been. The usual history-taking had been totally absent. I had no idea about his accident, his parents, his earlier life, his art, his losses, his hopes for the future—none at all. I felt I had worked hard with him—put in a lot of energy and been more active than I normally would have been in this mutual assessment with a client. In light of this, I even got to doubting my no-fee policy. But I returned to the more immediate and important matter of Charles. "We have only a few minutes left," I informed him. "We need to decide whether we feel we can work together or not. What do you think?"

"What do *you* think?" he echoed in response, but I simply held his gaze knowing, this time, I would not break eye contact. This definitely *was* the time for a game of chicken, though it really was no game. This was the very heart of his issue. He stared back. I could almost feel him willing me to declare my decision first. Tempting though it was to give him my answer, of course I would not. I gazed back at him and waited, face to face.

Tales out of school

Dear Maureen,

Thank you for your letter of 15th June. I was delighted to hear from you, and yes, of course, I remember meeting you at the "Serendipity in psychotherapy" conference. It was quite a memorable day for me too — in more ways than one.

I am somewhat surprised to learn of your beginning a psychotherapy training, remembering as I do your rather busy personal life, your counselling work, and your ongoing gynaecological problems — but good for you! I do hope your training course goes well and that you are enjoying the delight, fascination and reward of becoming a psychotherapist, despite the struggle with contemporary theory you seem to be having — in relation to which, you ask some probing questions of me as an older (by the way, I do prefer "older" to "elderly") practitioner in this postmodern world.

I shall endeavour to answer them with the candor you request of me. For your part, I ask simply that you take what I write as my current personal views and that you treat them as something merely to consider, play with, challenge, and refute in your quest for finding your own perspective. Be warned that I tend to loquaciousness when invited to pontificate on these matters. Luckily, you can merely stop reading and I'll never know.

It seems unbelievable (to me at least) that I've been a psychotherapist for about forty years and in that time must have worked with several hundreds of clients and read equally as many books on the subject of psychotherapy. I mention these facts not as a boast or an argument toward the necessity of my retirement but because, though I greatly enjoy both, the correlation between clients and theory often eludes me. I wonder if you have discovered this too and whether this is part of your feeling perplexed?

Of course, there's a modicum of theory in most of these volumes that sometimes makes sense in connection to actual clients (well, all human beings really) and is helpful to the therapeutic process but, more often than not these days, I find them worlds apart.

This may be something to do with me and my stage of life as a therapist — new theory (invariably old theory reformulated) arises at an alarming rate — but, while my ageing brain might simply be overwhelmed and confused, the strange thing is, it seems to me that most of the authors themselves struggle to make the connection between their theory and practice.

Their elaborate, often labyrinthine, expositions of their theories, requiring lengthy, esoteric, if not newly minted words, sometimes take me an enormous amount of time and effort to grasp, turning backward and forward to find out just where I lost the plot and if I can pick it up again.

Then, having persevered to roughly grasp the theory, I reach the chapter's concluding case vignette with relief and gratitude. At last the theory will come to life and all will be revealed. After all, that is what these examples are meant to do, is it not — to illustrate the preceding theory? It appears not. I'm not exaggerating when I say sometimes it's like reading a recipe for coq au vin illustrated by a picture of plum duff. Well, maybe I exaggerate slightly.

I'm loath to give you examples from these books, ubiquitous though they are, as I don't want to make my point at the expense of particular writers while others get off scot-free. But recently I read a lengthy paper about the influence of unconscious and primitive intrapsychic processes in generating co-created enactments within the phenomenological and intersubjective experience of the interpersonal therapeutic relationship (you see what I mean about the language).

Hoping you will forgive the vernacular, Maureen — my own paraphrasing of this would be: when my unresolved shit meets your unresolved shit and neither of us know we have shit, shit will happen (though I should say *might* happen, as unconscious processes, slippery customers that they are, defy certainty or prediction).

If the writer had written in this vein I'd have grasped the idea much sooner but so convoluted was the argument, so obfuscating the words, that it took me quite a while to reach this possibility, and even then I wasn't absolutely sure. My doubt was very much fuelled by the thought that, if this was really what was being said, I had just wasted valuable time and effort (not to mention money — good heavens, the price of books these days!) on a concept that your therapy training probably addressed in its introductory module.

Be that as it may, I reached the latter part of the paper where the case example promised to throw light on the matter. It did not.

By the time I'd read it, I was still in the dark, totally none the wiser.

The example began with a long case history of a young black woman whose alcoholic, single mother was at best negligent and at worst physically abusive. Really, given the interchange that follows, that's all the reader needed to know but the writer thought otherwise.

Page after page of descriptions of neglectful and abusive parenting at various ages and stages of this woman's life were presented, and I had the uncomfortable thought that perhaps the writer was gaining some sort of erotic, sadistic pleasure from dwelling on these awful details. Maybe this was some of his own unresolved shit of which, even in the writing of it, he remained unaware.

Eventually, we were invited into the consulting room. The client is talking of a recent relationship with an older white man in which, unsurprisingly given our human compulsion to repeat, she is neglected and physically abused.

The therapist, having been silent for the best part of the session (and failing to consider that perhaps this was a repeat of the mother's neglectful attitude to her daughter, a re-enactment that might have been useful to explore) says, "So you left this man rather than confront his behaviour?" And the client replies, "Yes." In response, the therapist (adding insult to injury, in my view) says, "I think this is a clear example of your avoidant attachment style" and goes on to describe how the client wept copiously at this interpretation. Q.E.D (in his view): she cried so I am right.

And that's where the case example ended, leaving me totally baffled. How on earth did this illustrate "the influence of unconscious and primitive intrapsychic processes", etcetera? Was he saying that her crying was an enactment? Why? And if so, where does he consider his part in this? What about his shit?

I certainly had the impression that this older, white, male therapist working with a young black woman had bucket loads of it. So much so that he had no clue that the client probably felt so judged and misunderstood by him that she could only weep in despair — which is pretty much what I felt on reading him. And I'm sure you do too.

Now, all this stuff you mention about unconscious processes: transference, countertransference, projection, introjection, splitting, unformulated experience, co-creation and so forth is all very well. It can be fascinating, engaging, challenging and humbling and sometimes illuminating — but only if it's seen as a possibility, and not as a truth.

What matters most is what the client makes of it and whether she or he finds anything in this perspective that might be useful. Sometimes it is, sometimes it isn't, and I think we therapists should be open to humbly accepting that sometimes we're barking up the wrong tree — like in the example I've just mentioned where I fear the therapist was barking in a totally different forest to his client and making gross assumptions about her that he didn't even bother to check out.

Which reminds me of a client I worked with many years ago, who shocked me by asking straight out at the start of a session if I was dying. Now, as her father had died when she was very young it was not too off-piste of me to assume that it was this event, and a fear of its repeat, that lay behind her question.

Thankfully, instead of automatically going along with this assumption and addressing her with a response to this effect, I simply enquired if she understood why she might be asking such a question. Only when she replied, "It's the blue stains on your fingers," did I register the other meaning of dying. I'd been blackberry-picking. My client was not at all concerned with my mortality.

Another situation comes to mind where, after about six months working together, a client on leaving a session said, "Goodbye Ian" but recognising his error, quickly corrected himself and said, "I mean Michael" as he closed the door behind him.

Being a trainee therapist himself, and well aware of projection, Freudian slips and the like, he spent the ensuing week puzzling over why he had made this mistake and who he might have been projecting on to me. We both explored it extensively next time we met but were at a loss.

He could recall no one named Ian from his past or present circumstances. Apart from the obvious exploration of his family, friends and neighbours, we played with famous Ians both current and historical and even infamous ones like Brady and Huntley. But we got nowhere. Despite the fact that this slip recurred several times in the four years we worked together, it remained a mystery.

I guess sometimes not only is a cigar just a cigar but a verbal slip is just a slip with no Freudian overtones (or should that be undertones?). Wouldn't it have been fascinating, had the Ian in question turned out to be Brady or Huntley, to explore my part in this co-created scenario? In the event, I was spared the task of unearthing my murderous fantasies.

You see, I'm not averse to the idea of co-creation, enactment, mutual relational influence, or whatever else it might be called. It makes sense to me that who I am and how I am in meeting with you, and who you are and how you are in meeting with me, will have some reciprocal effect.

A simple example would be any meeting between two people of the opposite sex. The immediate assumptions we make about each other based on our own individual experiences of anyone and everyone of the opposite sex inevitably effects our meeting in some way for good or ill.

But I do find difficulty in the notion of an ever-present and significant co-transference: the idea that both parties are always playing some part in the unconscious construction of a shared, important something — intersubjectivity running rampantly through everything. Bob immediately springs to mind but I'll come back to him in a moment because right now I feel a rant coming on and would be the better for getting it off my chest.

You see, in the past several years I've taken on a number of clients who I would describe as casualties of bogus intersubjectivity. By this I mean where therapists abuse the permission given by this concept to share their own feelings with the client.

It's all very well, with the client's agreement, to occasionally disclose a feeling, a discomfort, a hunch, or even an uncertainty in response to the client, but only if it's for the benefit of the client; only if the disclosure on the therapist's part remains client-centred. Which brings me to the "casualties" whose sessions have been hijacked by so many disclosures of the therapist's feelings that the poor clients have felt they were responsible for looking after him (and, I must say, it does seem to be the male therapists who are the culprits here. Perhaps they think that by expressing their feelings they're demonstrating just how evolved they are).

In other words, the dynamic has been turned totally on its head. The therapy has become therapist-centred. Many of these clients have complained to me of their therapists with heartfelt cries of "I didn't want to know what *he* was feeling, I wanted him to listen to me and *my* feelings!", and in voicing this to their therapists at the time had been accused of resistance or avoidance or acting out and, in one instance, of not being "psychodynamically literate enough" to be in therapy.

Hmm, so whatever happened to intersubjectivity? OK, I'm done on that one and I'm feeling very much the better for it.

Now back to Bob. Ah yes, this was to do with the notion of ever-present and significant co-transference; how everything going on between two people is co-created all the time.

Well, on one level, as I've indicated, this may be stating the obvious. I mean, I can't be in the presence of another person (unless I'm totally oblivious to their presence and they to mine) without some mutual awareness occurring; without some assumptions about the other taking place and having some effect upon the interaction.

For instance, take the acne-ridden young man on the overcrowded bus the other day, who had just looked up at me from his seat. He had probably correctly assessed that I'm getting on a bit and that I was thinking it was selfish of him to remain seated while I clung on precariously to the dangling thing. At the same time, his sitting there unmoving confirmed all my assumptions of spotty youth. I imagined he thought I shouldn't be travelling on buses at all at my age and that my travel card may have allowed me a free ride but it did not entitle me to a seat.

Now, I'll never be certain whether it was the scowl on my face or my inadvertently breaking wind or something else entirely (or nothing to do with me at all) that induced him to move to the other end of the bus, but perhaps one could say that co-creation had been wonderfully achieved as I took his vacated seat (though I have a feeling I've gone astray in this little story).

And talking of going astray — I've wandered from Bob again (which may or may not be something to do with Bob or a co-created something between us. It could purely be me and my brain cells diminishing by the minute. You will have to judge for yourself). Bob had a very fixed belief that other people hated him — his girlfriend, his staff, his friends, his postman — and, as you've probably guessed, this list included me.

From the off, he could see hatred in my eyes, in the way I sat, in the slightest flicker of an earlobe, and every nuance in my tone of voice — none of which seemed to me to bear any resemblance to reality. However hard I tried to find something in me that hated him, I just didn't. In actual fact, despite feeling occasionally frustrated by him, I rather liked him and wanted to engage with him, to get to know him and understand his paranoid way of seeing others.

Now, my supervisor at that time was very keen on co-creativity theory, and being an adaptive type of person (as you may have noted already) I explored any slight hint of hatred I might be harbouring against Bob with her and in my own personal therapy.

Did I resent him being half my age? No, I didn't — I was rather enjoying my senior years (and breaking wind on buses had yet to come). Did I hate him being in a relationship? Well, given I'd recently extricated myself from a relationship that had turned sour, no — I was enjoying my escape to freedom. Did I want, like him, to run a restaurant or watch cars racing? No, I did not — the first would mean unsocial hours and the second excited me less than watching a game of tiddlywinks. So it went on.

I even resorted to recording our sessions to see if I could hear hatred in my tone of voice, my inflections, my phraseology, my choice of words, but nothing came to light, and when I shared the recordings with Bob he could not hear any hatred either but maintained that the recordings distorted the quality of my voice — such was his determination to be hated.

Now, if this phenomena (with its origins, unsurprisingly, rooted in Bob's relationship with his mother, who did not to respond well to her unplanned seventh child and treated him harshly and critically from the start) had involved me and a few specific other people in his life, I might have continued searching even more assiduously for something in me and within my way of relating to Bob that was contributing to his belief that I hated him, as his mother had hated him.

But, as his belief involved everyone in his life — past, present and future (yes, he even

believed the people about to move in next
door, who he had yet to meet, hated him) —
I came to the conclusion that I was merely a
cardboard cut-out in Bob's projected world,
along with everyone else. Nothing special,
nothing co-created, no co-transference, just
projection pure and simple, which led to my
firm but gentle assertion, in response to yet
another accusation of hatred from Bob, that
I was not his mother and that any further
insistence on his part that I and others hated
him might indeed become a self-fulfilling
prophecy, as it had become already with his
girlfriend and the postman. This straightfor-
ward confrontation was just what Bob needed
to start reassessing his beliefs.

Sometimes therapist navel-gazing, however
well intended, can get in the way of helping
the client. Sometimes we need to leave ourselves out of it. Sometimes we're not that
important, and our theories even less so.
Though we may wish to feel more significant
than a cardboard cut-out, that's exactly what
our client may need us to be for a while.
Bob, like most of us some of the time, was
in his own head in his own inner world. The
outer world could have been the Sahara Desert
and he'd have maintained each grain of sand
hated him. Do I make my point?

Moving on (as I want to address all your
questions as best I can), you ask for my
understanding of "rupture and repair", which

142

always makes me think of the punctures in my bicycle tyres — and I guess the idea has some similarities, apart from tyres refusing to learn from the experience. It's based on the idea that as human beings in relationship we learn and develop through others getting it wrong and letting us down.

It's not the only way we learn and develop, thank goodness. It's just one way. And it very much depends on the relationship we've already formed with the person who at some point gets it wrong.

Thus, a toddler whose attentive father is invariably there to help her dress each morning is upset when he has to take an important phone call in the next room. Momentarily, she feels abandoned and frustrated. She cries a bit, but soon, drawing on the mass of other times that dad has been there for her, she soothes herself in the way he has done in the past (maybe even saying comforting things he's said to her). Now, not only does she feel better and more able to wait, she starts to dress herself. No matter that it's all rather haphazard; she just gets on with it. On his return, seeing she's been upset, dad apologises for having to take the call, gives her a cuddle, thanks her for waiting, and tells her how well she's done in getting dressed.

In this incident, she's learnt many things. She's developed her capacity to be alone for a few minutes, to self-soothe, to reinforce her trust in dad (that he'll be back), and, as an added bonus, to be independent in making a stab at getting dressed. Add to this those other occasions when a busy parent cannot attend immediately to a child's needs, and you can see how the child, forced onto her own capacities and past experience of others, furthers her own development incrementally.

So through rupture (dad having to take a phone call) and repair (her reconfiguring of her internal world, and dad returning and acknowledging her feelings and her achievements) the child develops. But only if it does not happen all the time. Too much rupture, even with attempted repair, will lead to stagnation, if not regression, rather than development.

So it is with significant others throughout our lives: we learn and we grow through the occasional rupture with our partners, family, friends, and therapists. But a word of caution: there's been an uncomfortable interpretation of this idea in psychotherapy in the past few years.

I've supervised several therapists who, according to them, have been taught on their training courses that they must "disturb" their clients each and every session. In other words, they must bring about a rupture that can then be repaired! And if their clients are not disturbed, the therapist is not doing psychotherapy! This is where theory, when applied badly, can become abusive. The theory of rupture and repair is not one that needs to be applied — it is a rather beautiful description of what happens, to a greater or lesser degree, quite naturally and spontaneously.

We're going to get things wrong for our clients — from our sessions not being long enough to holidays interrupting, from mishearing to totally misunderstanding what's being said, and being challenging when an empathic response may have been needed (and vice versa). The possibilities are endless. We certainly don't need to manufacture them! And, if we do, isn't any repair going to be equally as artificial and empty?

I wonder if your trainers and tutors are pushing this sort of nonsense at you? If so, I would suggest you disturb *them* a bit by questioning their authenticity and congruence in relation to their clients.

In my experience, the ones who bang on about "disturbance" in the same breath as "authentic", "intersubjective" and "relational" are often acting out their own problems in relating. They wouldn't know a relationship from a bar of soap — and that's why they need to stir up their clients until they create a bit of a lather. No advantage for the client but no doubt the therapist will feel met.

Oh dear, Maureen, this is all probably far too jaundiced a critique for someone like yourself about to launch into the wonderful world of psychotherapy, so let me end with something more positive.

I believe the privilege of working as a psychotherapist is a happy, challenging and creative one. Us human beings are diverse and fascinating creatures. Our lives are unique yet all share the existential challenge of birth and death and how we pass, spend, fill or fritter away the time in between. Our stories contain the originality of a work of art yet, like a painting, are framed and proscribed by the given elements. Within that frame, patterns emerge and it is the attention we give to these shared patterns, as well as to the uniqueness of each of our clients in relationship with us, that psychotherapy is all about.

Your greatest learning will be from your clients, but you ask for my advice on what to read. Well, obviously you'll be reading vast quantities of books on psychotherapy theory like the ones I referred to earlier, and I would encourage you to read them despite my reservations — just be critical and questioning of them.

However, my strongest advice is that you read novels — enjoy them, devour them, always have one on the go alongside your textbooks, for you will learn far more of the human condition from them than any theory. Fiction, after all, is probably the most reliable form of reality outside our own lives.

I wish you well.

Yours,
Michael Martin

Reflections

I hope these short stories have been enjoyable for you to read, simply as entertaining tales. Additionally, I hope you will enjoy reflecting on them to discover how they may be helpful to you in your learning and development as a therapist. Each of the stories raises issues and challenges that might be faced by any-one preparing to engage, or already engaged, in the practice of counselling and psychotherapy. Maybe you've been critically assessing the style and interventions of the therapist as you've been reading each story, and considering your own approach to these clients and the issues they present—in particular, iden-tifying what you would have done or said differently. To assist your personal considerations and to stimulate discussion with your peers and colleagues, I draw attention below to some of the key challenges of each story and provide some questions for you to reflect upon from your own theoretical perspective. Where appropriate, I suggest further reading to explore these issues in more detail, and refer to textbooks on specific theo-retical and technical aspects in which you may be interested.

If there is one belief I have tried to convey in these stories, it is that there is no single "right" way to work therapeutically with another person and that each unique dyad will find its own way to be together (perhaps, struggling to do so some of the time) for the benefit of the client.

Listen carefully

In the very first sentence of this story we get an idea of how the client, Holly, reacts to things: dramatically, angrily, rudely, and impulsively. A few sentences later she reappears: quietly, tentatively, apologetically, and politely. This marked alternation may suggest, in part, what in the psychotherapy literature would be described as a borderline personality adaptation. The story goes on to provide further indications that Holly's personality style might well be described in this way. Elinor Greenberg (1989) offers the mnemonic device MISERY to highlight issues presented by people with this adaptation, and I invite you to consider Holly and her story, and how the therapist responds to her, in relation to each of these:

> Mother problems: Failure to separate and individuate, emotionally craving attention and approval, repetition of these dynamics in adult relationships.
>
> Identity problems: Who am I? Which of the unintegrated, sometimes contradictory, aspects of myself is me?
>
> Splitting: People (and oneself) are either totally good or totally bad, or all good one minute and all bad the next.
>
> Engulfment and abandonment fears: Originating in relationship to the primary caretaker's inappropriate and oscillating demands, and leading to alternately withdrawing and clinging behaviours.
>
> Rage: Anger and hostility that feels boundless, uncontrollable, and destructive.
>
> Yearning: For the special, perfect other who will give total, unconditional love.

I would also recommend further reading on the borderline personality adaptation in the works of Johnson (1994), who in his book *Character Styles* refers to this as the symbiotic character style; Otto Kernberg's *Borderline Conditions and Pathological Narcissism* (1975) and *Severe Personality Disorders* (1984); Jerold Kreisman and Hal Strauss's *I Hate You—Don't Leave Me* (1989); James Masterson's *The Search for the Real Self* (1988); and James Masterson and Anne Lieberman's *A Therapist's Guide to the Personality Disorders* (2004).

It appears that at some point in the therapy the therapist had shared with Holly some breathing techniques for self-regulation that Holly employs on her return to the therapy room (pp. 3–4) and that the therapist himself uses a while later (p. 7).

- Is this something you might use with your clients?
- Is it something you might find useful for yourself when working with clients or in general?
- Do you think there is any relationship between breathing and emotional or psychological regulation? If so, how do you understand this?

In relation to Holly's sexual encounters, the therapist (p. 4) appears to be disapproving, judgemental, and opinion-giving. Indeed, he admits to finding it difficult to stay neutral with Holly, though this is always his intention. By the same token, a while later, the therapist says that "sometimes it was hard to resist responding to Holly's provocations" but in light of Holly's "tendency towards impulsivity rather than thought", he knows she needed him "to remain calm and non-attacking" (p. 7).

- Why do you think the therapist intends to stay neutral, calm and non-attacking, particularly with Holly? What might be the problem if he is not?

- Would you have difficulty staying neutral with Holly? If so, what is it about her that you might find difficult in this respect?
- Do you agree with Holly that the therapist is "not supposed to disapprove" (p. 4)? If so, why? If not, in what circumstances might you express your disapproval of a client's behaviour?
- How do you understand the principle of holding a non-judgemental attitude towards clients? How would you explain this and its therapeutic purpose to a layperson?

It becomes apparent that Holly, until recently, has had a history of overdosing, and self-harming through cutting her arms (pp. 7–8). In his belief that they are more attention-seeking and manipulative than life-threatening, the therapist has never remarked upon either of these behaviours (p. 8). His strategy appears to be working but …

- What do you think of his strategy?
- What are the potential risks of taking this position, and how would you assess whether or not to take such risks?
- Is this a strategy that would work for all clients who were self-harming or overdosing? What would be your exceptions or objections to this strategy?
- In her paper "Signing with a scar", Gillian Straker (2006) presents the subjective experiences of people who cut themselves, and explores the conscious and unconscious meanings of this phenomenon. Her thesis goes beyond a self-soothing function towards a more intersubjective and relational striving, which, though ineffective in itself without relationship, is a step along the way to finding an intersubjective self. What is your understanding of self-harming behaviour?
- Following a pivotal session with Holly in which she realises her "wrecking" behaviour is an ineffective attempt to be

loved and cared for by her mother (pp. 10–11), she turns her attention to calmer pursuits. However, the therapist is concerned that these will not satisfy Holly's need for excitement and incident (p. 11). Eric Berne (1972) describes these human needs as *hungers*—for stimulus, recognition, and structure. These can be added to or rather subdivided into our hunger for relationship, contact, sexual fulfilment, and incident (see also Lapworth & Sills, 2011). Individuals have different levels of need in these areas. In the story, Holly's "incident hunger" is satisfied by hang-gliding, while the therapist's is satisfied by an annual trip to the seaside. On a scale of 1 to 10, where would you assess your own level of hunger in the following?

Incident and excitement
Social contact
Physical contact
Sexual contact
Acknowledgement and recognition from others
Structured time.

- Do you manage to satisfy these hungers to these levels?
- If you assess your clients' or friends' levels of hunger using the same scale, and then consider their satisfaction levels, how do they achieve?
- If your assessments of your own, your clients' or your friends' levels of satisfaction do not meet the levels of need, why do you think this is and what can you or they do about it?

Concerned after his enforced absence and Holly's failure to resume her sessions, the therapist phones her but is left feeling disturbed by their conversation. He is ambivalent about her return and says "To my shame, in my hurt and anger at Holly's response, I felt her mother's selfish love and toxic hate rise in me with the force of a tsunami" (p. 15).

- How do you view what could be seen as a breaking of boundaries when the therapist not only phones his client but also offers a session outside their normal time (p. 15)? What might be the pros and cons of such boundary violations?
- How did you feel when you read of the therapist's powerful response to Holly at the end of the phone call (p. 15)?
- How might *your* feeling response have shed some light upon the dynamics that were occurring between therapist and client?
- What is your understanding of the transference and countertransference (the hidden dynamics) occurring between them?
- In supervision, the therapist recognises that he and Holly share mothers who use their children as "alternating carers and combatants in a bid to meet their own unmet needs of childhood" (p. 16). In your approach to therapy, how would you describe this and how would you conceptualise the two understandings the therapist then reaches?

In her book, the *Therapeutic Relationship in Psychoanalysis, Counselling and Psychotherapy* (1995, p. 63), Petruska Clarkson provides a helpful summary table of transference (and countertransference) phenomena. As a useful introduction to transference and countertransference, I would recommend Brendan McLoughlin's *Developing Psychodynamic Counselling* (1995) and, for further exploration, David Mann and Valerie Cunningham's *The Past in the Present* (2009) and Karen Maroda's *The Power of the Countertransference* (2004).

In response to Holly's misunderstanding that he had cancelled his therapy sessions "on a whim", the therapist does not initially correct her, being of the opinion that "her experience was more important than whatever had happened to me" (p. 18). However, some time later in their exchange, realising that Holly believes he has taken a "holiday at the drop of a hat" (p. 19), he decides that not telling her the real reason is "tantamount to lying" and "an unnecessary and unkind manipulation" (p. 19).

- How do you understand the therapist's change of heart? What do you think had occurred that might explain what appears like a contradiction?
- In your opinion, should a client's misassumptions go unchallenged or be allowed to persist, and how would you justify taking either of these positions?
- Perhaps your answer to the above is "it depends". But upon what? In what circumstances might you choose to do one or the other?

The end of the story finds both therapist and client laughing convulsively, and the therapist asserts his belief that laughter and humour have "a rightful and important place in the consulting room" (pp. 20–21).

- Do you agree? Why?
- When do you think laughter and humour might be therapeutically appropriate and when might they be inappropriate, even damaging?

Uncoupled

Admitting to his tendency to take sides when working with couples, the therapist has stopped doing such work, suggesting it would be unethical (p. 23), untenable, and a disservice (p. 24).

- Do you agree with his judgement and that when working with couples neutrality is a crucial quality (p. 23)?
- If so, why do you make this judgement?
- Why do you or why do you not hold neutrality as crucial?

Reflections

- Given the human tendency to side with people we like or admire more than others, how would you deal with your own "taking sides" when working with couples (or even when with your partnered friends)?
- The therapist favours people who express their feelings over those who "lived life in their head" (p. 24). If you had preferences for certain qualities in people, what would they be? Again, how would you manage these qualitative preferences when working with couples?

For anyone interested in an integrative approach to working with couples, I recommend Maria Gilbert and Diana Shmukler's *Brief Therapy with Couples* (1996), and for couples interested in practical guidance, Sarah Litvinoff's *The Relate Guide to Better Relationships* (2001).

The therapist names some of the games and pastimes played by couples—"*Ain't it awful*', '*I always … she never …*", "*If it weren't for you*"—most of which come from Eric Berne's witty and unnerving book *Games People Play* (1964) where he recognises that, at times, we all communicate indirectly with each other via ulterior transactions, moving towards a "payoff" that is repetitive and predictable. Further to Berne's book, I would recommend Phil Lapworth and Charlotte Sills' *An Introduction to Transactional Analysis* (2011) and Ian Stewart and Vann Joines' *TA Today* (1987) both of which explore game theory in some detail.

- In your experience of working with couples, what are some of the psychological games you have observed being played?
- Equally, if you are in a couple, what are the games that you and your partner play most frequently?
- If, like Berne, you gave these games pithy titles, what would they be?

- With your clients (or within your personal relationships), what ways have you discovered to help avoid playing games?

The therapist suggests (1) that it is unacknowledged needs and desires in relationships that lead to game playing, (2) that those needs could be generalised under the term "love", and (3) that those love-related needs for "attention, recognition, understanding, acceptance" (pp. 25–26) (often played out through games in the present) are deficits from childhood.

- With which of these three statements do you agree or disagree?
- On what experience, theories or general understandings do you base your agreement or disagreement?

I once commented to a stranger at a party that the long-standing couple whose party it was seemed very happy and well-suited. Then I added—regrettably as it turned out— "They must have had good-enough parents". The stranger didn't understand what I meant at all, nor did I manage to persuade him of the possible connection between childhood and adulthood (including the way we relate) despite a lengthy discussion.

- How would you have explained how we bring the past into the present and how our current relationships might reflect those of our childhood?
- Which particular theories do you employ to understand this phenomenon?
- What evidence from clinical or neuroscientific research do you draw upon to back up your chosen theories?
- How do these theories apply in your own relationships?

In this and other stories, the therapist refers to personality disorders (p. 26) and adaptations or styles (p. 69). He even attempts (unsuccessfully) to invent one of his own for his client. Stephen Johnson (1994) suggests a continuum from style to disorder along which we all might place ourselves according to the severity of the patterns of our ways of being in the world. Throughout the psychiatric and psychotherapeutic literature, these patterns, or diagnostic classifications, with their (for the most part) distinctive clusters of issues, expressions and ways of relating to others are referred to in such terms as schizoid, histrionic, narcissistic, obsessive compulsive, and so on (see DSM-5, 2013 and ICD-10, 1992).

- Do you think of your clients in these terms?
- If so, how is this useful in your approach to therapeutic work with clients? If not, are you simply not familiar with them, or do you consider them to be unhelpful?
- What are the pros and cons of what could be seen as "label-ling" your clients in this way?
- How do you feel about placing yourself in one or more of these categories? Why?

"She sent me here," says the client, Victor, concluding his several complaints of his wife (p. 27). In response, the therapist "was sure there was no point in working with someone who'd been sent by his wife" (p. 28).

- Do you agree with the therapist? Why?
- How would you respond to a client who had been "sent" by someone else?
- Are there any circumstances in which you would or would not see this as a problem? What might they be?
- How would you respond if you suspected a client was inventing something (in Victor's case, "I want to be more

confident" (p. 28)) simply to placate the third party by whom she or he had been sent?

- How would you work with someone whose focus is on complaining about others?

Initially, the therapist "felt rather repulsed" by Victor (p. 27). Later, on learning of his mother's "wicked and violent behaviour towards him" (p. 31), he feels "sad and ashamed at my lack, until this moment, of empathy" (p. 31).

- Perhaps you have not had such an extreme initial reaction as this therapist, but how have you managed any strong, negative feelings you may have had towards a client?
- Whether negative or positive, what do your unusually strong responses indicate to you? How do you work with such feelings?
- In your experience, what have been the change moments for you when working with clients with whom you initially found it difficult to empathise?
- Have you ever worked with a client with whom you found it impossible to be empathic? If yes, why do think this was and what did you do about this? If not, what do you think you would do in such circumstances?

Prior to the disastrous denouement of this story, the therapist owns up to his initial critical and judgemental attitude towards Victor (pp. 32–33), seeing this as a session "in which we both authentically responded to each other, intimate in our confession of our experience of each other" (p. 34).

- In your model or approach to therapy, how would you describe this aspect of the therapist-client relationship?
- What is your opinion of the therapist disclosing his judgemental thoughts and fearful feelings to his client? What

might be the pitfalls of this approach? (See the final story, Tales Out of School, p. 129.)

- How do you view "authenticity" and "intimacy" within the therapeutic relationship? Are there circumstances in which you would consider such relating to be inappropriate? When? How would you relate differently?

The therapeutic relationship has been deemed a significant and positive determining factor in counselling and psychotherapy (see Cooper, 2008), and the "real" relationship (see Gelso & Carter, 1985) is seen as an important part of this, particularly within more humanistic approaches. But there has been a specific "relational turn" in psychotherapy in general, and contemporary psychoanalysis in particular, over the last couple of decades, and I would point the interested reader to Patricia DeYoung's *Relational Psychotherapy: A Primer* (2003), Martha Stark's *Modes of Therapeutic Action* (1999), and Paul Wachtel's *Relational Theory and the Practice of Psychotherapy* (2008) as very useful introductions.

Woody Bay

In this session with Emily, his elderly and terminally ill client, the therapist follows her meandering reminiscences with little intervention. He listens to her story and they sit together in silence quite frequently. Their thoughts seem sometimes to be synchronous (pp. 38–39).

- Do you consider this to be therapy? If so, how would you justify it as being therapy? If not, what would you describe it as, and do you see a place for it in the consulting room? Where might it be more appropriate?
- When working with clients, of any age and health, does silence have a value or purpose between you? When might it be therapeutic? When might it not be appropriate or useful?

- In silences, do you sometimes feel a need to intervene—to fill the space? If so, what is usually going on for you at that time?
- What do you think of the contract "to support her in 'living towards death'" (p. 37)? Is this a contract you would agree to make in similar circumstances? Why or why not?
- Have you had experiences where your unspoken thoughts have coincided synchronously with what your client is thinking about? How do you understand this?
- There are times when the therapist seems confident ("I have no intention of stopping her, p. 38), but at other times he is unsure ("It feels disingenuous of me, like I'm playing some sort of game with reality", p. 39); again with regards to the value of his client retelling her story of adolescent love that he has apparently heard many times before ("I begin to doubt the usefulness of this particular reminiscence", p. 42). What do you consider to be the value in her retelling of her story?
- How would you justify the therapist's occasional dishonesty in encouraging a story he knows already?

Though he is aware and admiring of "the impact she has had upon the world, the invaluable legacy she is leaving" (p. 41) and tempted to comment on her positive influence (p. 42), he does not draw on these facts to counterbalance her sadness and sense of unfulfilment (p. 48).

- Why do you think the therapist does not remind Emily of all the positive achievements she has made in her life? Would you have done? Why or why not?
- Equally, the therapist could perhaps have encouraged her more to stay with the positive aspects of her adolescent story and not let her continue to the end (p. 46). Would you have done this? Why or why not?

The therapist believes Emily's grief will accompany her to the end; that life is changed by losses and can never be the same—that "they are holes in our very being" (p. 47).

- What do you think he means by this last statement?
- Do you agree with it or do you consider that a grieving process eventually leads to our losses being integrated in some way; that they will fade with time?
- Which models or approaches to grieving have you been taught in your training and which make most sense to you?
- What do you consider might be different about the way you work with an elderly person as opposed to someone younger? What might be the particular factors you need to take into account?
- What about with a terminally ill client? How do think your approach and style of working would be different to that with someone apparently physically healthy? How would it differ specifically?

The poem the therapist struggles to remember at the beginning of the story (p. 38) is "Here" by R. S. Thomas, and the Virginia Woolf quote about islands of light (p. 40) is from her poetic novel *The Waves*. For those interested in approaches to working with older people, I refer you to *The Therapeutic Purposes of Reminiscence* (1999) by Mike Bender, Paulette Bauckham, and Andrew Norris; *Reminiscence & Life Story Work* (2011) by Faith Gibson; and, with regards to addressing loss and dying, *On Death and Dying* (1970) by Elisabeth Kubler-Ross and *Loss and Grief* (2002) edited by Neil Thompson.

Super vision

In this story, the therapist is in a supervision session with his supervisor (who does seem to have some super vision), focusing on his therapy with Sophie. All student counsellors and psychotherapists on recognised UK training courses as well as qualified practitioners registered, for example, with the United Kingdom Council for Psychotherapy (UKCP), the British Association for Counselling and Psychotherapy (BACP) or the

British Psychological Society (BPS) are required to have their clinical work supervised on a regular basis.

- Whether a student or experienced practitioner, what is the importance and value of supervision to you?
- What are you wanting from supervision? Do you get it? If not, why and how can you change this?
- If you could only have three of the following in your supervision sessions—guidance, encouragement, direction, support, exploration, advice, discussion, teaching, modelling, creativity—which would you choose and why?
- Which of the following areas of your work do you take regularly to supervision?

  1. An overview of your current clients: numbers, range of problems, frequency of sessions, length of therapy, etc.
  2. Your clients' histories, their emotional, psychological and behavioural problems, diagnoses, developmental and relational needs.
  3. The relationship between you and your clients.
  4. Your emotional response to your clients.
  5. The unconscious process between you and your clients.
  6. Your stuckness and difficulties with your clients.
  7. Your successes with your clients.
  8. Treatment planning.
  9. Theoretical considerations.
  10. Ethical dilemmas.
  11. Your own continuing professional development needs.
  12. Your self-care and personal current issues.
  13. Administration of your practice.

In the story, the therapist says he has presented in supervision those clients who "had pressed preferentially for time and attention by the greater degree of difficulty I was experiencing with them" (p. 49).

- As with his client, Sophie, do some of your clients get overlooked in the supervision of your practice? Who are they likely to be? What steps can you take to reduce the possibility of such oversight?
- Do you have one or two clients who seem to demand a great deal of supervisory attention? What are the potential implications of this for you, for your supervisor, for these clients, and for your remaining clients? What might you need to do to change this situation?
- How do you select which clients to take to supervision?
- Though a client may never know whether or not they are discussed in supervision, the therapist here suggests that because *he* will know "this could affect our work together, however subtly" (p. 49). Do you agree? If so, what has been your experience of this subtle (or not so subtle) influence? Why do you think this phenomenon occurs?
- The supervisor uses a technique of asking the therapist "If Sophie was an animal, what would she be?" I know this party game as "If It's ..." where only one person knows the identity of the secretly chosen person while others guess who she might be from the answers to their questions. What do think of this variation on the game being used in supervision? Do you think it might be a useful and creative technique for you to use? If so, why? If not, why not?
- When using this technique, why might it be important to be spontaneous (p. 49) and not let judgements get in the way (p. 50)?
- What purpose might such a technique have? In this story, what do you notice that might indicate its potential in learning about Sophie and the therapist's work with her?
- A parallel process often occurs in supervision where the therapist's response to the supervisor mirrors the client's response to the therapist. Where in the story do you find some parallel processes occurring?

- Equally, by her way of being with the supervisee, a supervisor (consciously or unconsciously) may model potential ways that the supervisee might helpfully relate, as therapist, to his client. Where in this story do you find such modelling occurring?
- Do you think that parallel processes and modelling could also contain some of the negative dynamics of the therapeutic relationship? How might these manifest in supervision? How do you think they might need to be worked with to be useful to you as the therapist?

For those readers interested in further considerations of supervision, I recommend Michael Carroll's *Effective Supervision for the Helping Professions* (2014), Maria Gilbert and Kenneth Evans' *Psychotherapy Supervision: An Integrative, Relational Approach to Supervision* (2000) and Peter Hawkins and Robin Shohet's *Supervision in the Helping Professions* (4th edition, 2012). Michael Carroll and Maria Gilbert have also written specifically for the supervisee: *On Being a Supervisee: Creating Learning Partnerships* (2nd edition, 2011).

In his *Psychanalytic Studies of the Personality* (1952, pp. 39–40), W. R. D. Fairbairn writes, "Frustration of his desire to be loved as a person and to have his love accepted is the greatest trauma that a child can experience". Reflecting on this in relation to Sophie's mother's response of "I don't love you, nobody loves you and no one ever will" to Sophie's "I love you mummy" (pp. 54–55), it is perhaps not surprising that the therapist refers to it as a "curse". But …

- These are strong words—"trauma" and "curse". Are they words that you would apply to this repeated experience between Sophie and her mother? How would you justify using them? What meaning do they have for you?
- Do you consider the word "trauma" to be overused in counselling and psychotherapy? Why or why not?

- How do you identify those clients who may have suffered, and continue to suffer, from trauma?
- What theories do you find helpful in relation to trauma, and what do you understand by the term "developmental trauma"?
- Some "multiple purposes" are suggested in the story in relation to Sophie's obsessions and compulsive rituals that started in childhood and continue into adulthood (p. 55). Do you agree with them? Do you have other hypotheses that could throw light on the development and maintenance of obsessions and rituals?
- What therapeutic approach would you take in working with someone who has developed obsessive-compulsive thoughts and behaviours?

On page 57, there is reference to a "rule of thumb" about addressing the thinking, feeling and behaviour (in that order) of people who have an obsessive-compulsive character style. This originates in the work of Paul Ware (1983), who suggests different orders of thinking, feeling and behaviour for different personality adaptations. This approach is helpfully described and illustrated in Vann Joines and Ian Stewart's *Personality Adaptations* (2002), and again I would recommend Stephen Johnson's *Character Styles* (1994) with reference to the obsessive-compulsive style as well as other character styles.

Different again

This story finds the therapist attempting to work with his client's current experience of racism. Their racial difference is obvious. It's literally black and white, and the white therapist, from the start, questions his black client, Junior, about how he feels about this. Later, not getting to grips with the racist issue, the therapist considers that maybe he needs a black supervisor to help explore his own racism or that maybe Junior needs a black therapist (p. 64).

- Do you think a black supervisor would have been a good idea? What would have been the advantages or disadvantages of this?
- Despite his client's reassurance that he wants a white therapist (p. 61), do you think the therapist should have referred him on to a black therapist? Why or why not?
- If you have worked with clients from different racial backgrounds to you, how has this difference enhanced or hindered the therapy?
- How about your work with clients who have been different to you in other ways: their age, sex, sexuality, gender identity, physical abilities, class, religion, relationship status, parenting status, and so on? What was this like for you? What were the aspects that you found particularly difficult or useful about your differences when working together?
- Did you address your obvious differences (sex, race, age) openly from the start? Did it become figural later, or did it not get mentioned at all throughout the therapy? Why or why not?
- How about your non-obvious differences (sexuality, religion, parenting status)? Have you sometimes thought it appropriate or important to disclose these aspects of yourself? When and why?
- If your client made an assumption that you are gay, or older than you are, or in a relationship or a Muslim, etc. (when you are not), would you correct their mistake? Why or why not?
- If you have referred any clients to other therapists for reasons of difference, what was your motivation and rationale for so doing?

Reflections

A training course that the therapist seems to rate as dealing well enough with issues of difference is mentioned (p. 65) but the therapist is aware that "in any profession people struggle with discrimination" (p. 64). He asserts that "everyone has prejudiced attitudes at some time or other because we all fear difference" (p. 64) and hopes that "in the psychotherapy world we explore these tendencies and try to understand and transform them" (p. 64).

- How do you rate your own therapy training in relation to working with difference? Was there enough time dedicated to such diversity issues? Was there a focus on a wide range of issues of difference? What would have improved your training regarding working with difference?
- In your training, personal development or therapy, have you explored your own prejudices towards different others? How have you undertaken this? What has been most useful to you? What prejudices do you continue to have and how do you understand your difficulty in working through them?
- Do you agree with the therapist in the story that our prejudices and oppressive attitudes towards others stem from our fear of difference? If so, how do you understand this and how does your theoretical model or approach explain this internal/interpersonal/cultural dynamic?
- How would you work with a client who is overtly racist, sexist, ageist, etc.? Would you always confront these prejudices? When, when not, and why?
- How did you react when you got to the end of the story? How do you understand your reaction? How did you feel about Junior, the therapist, and the writer?
- Despite (or perhaps because of) having suffered racism throughout his life, Junior appears (p. 74) to have racist attitudes himself. Potentially, what in the story might have

indicated this denouement? How might you understand his "colourist" racist attitude?

- One could see this as a form of internalised racism. In the same way, a gay client may bring their internalised homophobia, a woman client her internalised sexism, or an elderly client his internalised ageism. Are you aware of your own and your clients' internalised oppression? How might you work with this personally and with your clients?
- What is your reaction when you hear a black person refer to themselves in a derogatory way concerning their race, or a gay person describe themselves as "straight-acting" or a woman claim (as I heard on the radio only this week) that women should expect the occasional "groping" from men (as she did when she was at work)? If they were your clients, would you confront them about their self-oppression? Why or why not?
- In your view, do political issues like these have a place in the personal space of the consulting room? Why or why not?
- Why do you think the therapy world (a) is dominated by whites (b) contains a majority of women practitioners yet is run by men in positions of power and (c) is populated mostly by middle-class people?

The therapist recalls the words of a former supervisor who'd said "It doesn't matter if what your client is bringing seems utter nonsense to you. It doesn't matter if you consider their story a total confabulation. It doesn't matter that they've seen fairies at the bottom of the garden or green Martians in the high street. What matters is that you listen and accept that this is their experience" (pp. 65–66).

- Do you agree with this statement or not?
- What might you see as the potential problems with such an assertion?

- Might it be a useful, general rule of thumb to hold lightly? If so, when might you decide *not* to use it?
- How have you handled situations with clients in which you have doubted the reality or authenticity of what they are telling you?
- If a client was to talk of "fairies at the bottom of the garden or green Martians in the high street," what would you do? Would you "listen and accept their experience" (p. 66) as suggested by the supervisor? If not, what would you do?

The therapist says that in their work together they "time travelled back and forth between his current experiences and his formative ones" (p. 69) and he refers to "out there" and "back then" to describe this. These are two aspects of Menninger's (1958) "triangle of insight": the third being "in here" (what goes on between the therapist and client in the therapy room). It is this aspect with which the therapist is struggling: to bring the possible racism between them into the room (p. 71).

- Whether you are familiar with the triangle of insight or not, do you monitor these three aspects in some way when working with your clients? How does your model or approach describe these three situational/temporal aspects?
- How would you explain to a layperson the purpose and therapeutic value of linking what is happening in a client's current situation with what went on in the past?
- Equally, how would you explain to a layperson the point of focusing on what is happening in the relationship between you and your client?
- Why do you think the therapist was so keen to explore what was going on between him and his client, particularly in relation to racism?
- How do you understand the therapist's realisation that he, like Junior, was perhaps "keeping his head down" (p. 71) in an "anything for a quiet life" kind of way (p. 71)? How

would you describe this shared dynamic? How would it fit on the triangle of insight?

For further exploration of issues of diversity, I would refer you to Colin Lago and Barbara Smith's *Anti-Discriminatory Practice in Counselling and Psychotherapy* (2nd edition, 2010) and Sue Wheeler's *Difference and Diversity in Counselling: Contemporary Psychodynamic Perspectives* (2006); in relation to racial and cultural diversity, Frank Lowe's *Thinking Space: Promoting Thinking about Race, Culture, and Diversity in Psychotherapy and Beyond* (2014) and Judy Ryde's *Being White in the Helping Professions* (2009). For those interested in learning more about "colourism" (where people of colour discriminate against each other according to their differing shades of colour), I refer you to Marita Golden's *Don't Play in the Sun: One Woman's Journey Through the Color Complex* (2005). In relation to working with sexuality and gender diversity, I would recommend Dominic Davies and Charles Neal's *Therapeutic Perspectives on Working with Lesbian, Gay and Bisexual Clients* (2000), Charles Neal and Dominic Davies' *Issues in Therapy with Lesbian, Gay, Bisexual and Transgender Clients* (2000), and for her perspective on homophobia and its internalisation, Carole Shadbolt's *Homophobia and Gay Affirmative Transactional Analysis* (2004).

The thrownness of life

"Thrownness" is a term used by the existential philosopher Martin Heidegger (1926) to refer to the fact that existence is thrown into being by chance, completely arbitrarily, just like throwing a dice. As Anna's story illustrates, we have no choice over our parents or the social, geographical, historical or cultural contexts into which we are born. I hope it further illustrates (by her survival through her traumatic childhood, her continuing existence, her search for meaning through relationship, and her endeavours to enhance her life) that though these givens of birth cannot be changed, our response to them can. Sadly for Anna, despite being courageous in her response (as the therapist sees her, p. 76), life appears to continue to "throw" things at her relentlessly to the very end.

- Do you agree with this existential, philosophical view of the thrownness of life? If so how do you support your view? If not, what arguments do you draw upon to refute it and what different or opposing philosophical (or, perhaps, religious) beliefs do you hold about life, its nature, and its meaning?
- How do your philosophical beliefs and assumptions about life and human "being" inform and influence your therapy practice?
- How did these philosophical beliefs and assumptions influence your choice of the approach to therapy in which you have trained? In what way does your model or approach support your personal beliefs and values?
- At one point, the angry therapist sees Anna's terminal cancer as inevitable (p. 85). Do you consider her illness and the outcome of this story to be inevitable? How would you support your view?
- How do you deal with your clients' and your own thoughts and feelings when life seems unfair?

The therapist questions whether their work together was "therapy as most people would understand it" (p. 77). There are times when he seems to be teaching Anna rather than doing therapy (pp. 77–78). At other times, he is directive in telling her what to do (p. 83), allows her to phone before sessions for support (p. 81), and contemplates accompanying her in her car to Bristol (p. 86).

- How do you understand "therapy"? Does simply being therapeutic in the consulting room warrant the description "therapy"? Do you consider the work in which Anna and her therapist engage to qualify as therapy? Why or why not?

- How would you justify "chatting" (pp. 77, 84) having a place in the consulting room? When and how might it be appropriate or not? What might be the pitfalls of chatting?
- The therapist's rationale for chatting is that he is teaching Anna conversational skills (p. 77) but what place has teaching in the consulting room?
- Have there been times when you have taught your client a behavioural skill, a relaxation technique, or something that might be considered outside the bounds of therapy? What was your rationale for doing this? How did you and your client negotiate this? What might be the advantages and disadvantages of teaching in therapy?
- In response to Anna's physical symptoms, the therapist insists she visit her GP (p. 83). As her symptoms worsen, he suggests this again (p. 85). How would you justify the therapist being directive in this way?
- Have you advised, suggested or insisted on a client obtaining an outside consultation or treatment of some sort? What? How did you reach this decision? Have there been times when this turned out to be not such a good idea? When and how come?
- If your client who suffers from panic attacks wanted to phone you for support on their journey to your consulting room (p. 81), would you give your permission or not? What would your reasons be?
- The therapist, at one point, contemplates helping Anna to drive to Bristol as her passenger (p. 86). What is your opinion of this? What part does her terminal illness play in your thinking? Without this extreme situation, would there ever be an occasion that you might do the same? When and why or why not?

- The therapist regrets that he never went to Bristol with Anna, saying "I should have travelled literally that extra mile with her" (p. 88). Have there been times when you have (or have not) walked the extra mile with your client? In what way? What was the outcome of this? According to Mick Cooper's *Essential Research Findings*, (2008, p. 109, Box 6.2) research suggests that "going the extra mile" has positive meaning for clients in feeling genuinely cared about and may also help form and strengthen the therapeutic alliance. But what do you see as problematic about going the extra mile with clients and how might you create safeguards against such problems?
- What was your reaction to the therapist saying to Anna, "I think you are truly amazing"? (p. 87) Why do you think he said it? Would you say such a thing to a client of yours (maybe you have)? Why or why not? What might be the pitfalls of such a warm and spontaneous exclamation?

Payment for Anna's therapy sessions is an issue from the start (p. 76). It is clear she cannot afford this therapist's usual hourly fee so he offers her a reduced one (p. 76). This is renegotiated upwards later in the therapy (p. 80). In light of her terminal illness the therapist ponders "I knew, without doubt, I would work with her to the end of her life. I determined that even if she could not pay, I would continue to see her every week" (pp. 85–86).

- As a practitioner, how do you decide how much to charge for a therapy session? What are the personal and professional factors that inform your decision?
- You hear of a therapist with less qualifications and experience running a thriving practice in your area and charging twice your fees. What do you do in response to this? Why and why not?

- Do you offer, or negotiate, lower fees than your usual hourly rate to some clients? If so, who might they be and what are the circumstances that would influence your decision? If not, what are your reasons for charging the same rate to all clients?
- Whether paying your normal fee or a reduced one, if your client's financial circumstances improved, would you renegotiate a higher fee? How would you approach this with your client and how would you decide how much the increase should be?
- If your client's financial situation worsened during their time in therapy with you, would you negotiate a lower fee, explore ways in which they could earn more, stop the therapy until their finances had improved, or work with them for nothing? How would you justify your decision?
- The therapist in the story believes he would continue to work with Anna without payment to the end of her life. Would you? Why or why not?

Anna has been sexually exploited and abused in childhood by both her parents, which, with no one to say otherwise, she thought was what most children experienced (p. 79).

- How might you explain how someone could be abused (either sexually, physically, or psychologically) and consider it normal? Are there aspects of your approach and theory of therapy that might help in explaining this?
- When the therapist suggests, "Her only saving grace was that she had little understanding of the aberrancy of what was happening to her" (p. 80), what do you think he means? Do you agree with him? Why or why not?
- The therapist adds that "although on many levels she did not understand … her body knew." Again, what do you think he means by this? How do you explain how one's body

can "know" something. What in your model or approach addresses this concept?

- The story does not deal specifically with how the therapist approached or worked with Anna in relation to her sexual abuse. Do you consider he was, nonetheless, implicitly addressing this issue? What approach do you take when addressing and working with sexual abuse and other traumatic experiences your clients may have suffered?

For the reader interested in learning more of existential philosophy in existential counselling and psychotherapy, I would recommend Hans Cohn's *Existential Thought and Therapeutic Practice* (1997), Mick Cooper's *Existential Therapies* (2003), Emmy van Deurzen's *Existential Counselling in Practice* (1988) and Ernesto Spinelli's *The Interpreted World* (1989). Exploring the origins and purpose of counselling and psychotherapy and what therapists do, I would suggest Norman Claringbull's *What is Counselling and Psychotherapy?* (2010) and for the management (including financial) of a therapy practice, Gladeana McMahon, Stephen Palmer, and Christine Wilding's *The Essential Skills for Setting Up a Counselling and Psychotherapy Practice* (2005). For those interested in approaches to working with trauma, I would recommend Kim Etherington's *Trauma, the Body and Transformation* (2003), Bessel van der Kolk's *The Body Keeps the Score: Brain, Mind and Body in the Healing of Trauma* (2014), Babette Rothschild's *The Body Remembers* (2000), and Christiane Sanderson's *Counselling Adult Survivors of Child Sexual Abuse* (2006).

Armadillo

The title of this story symbolises the therapist's view of his client, Chris, who in his outward appearance and behaviour seems to be confident and thickly armoured, protected against the possibility of anything penetrating beneath the surface to his vulnerability. Yet something has broken through his defence: his desire for intimacy with Maria. Though presenting with the problem of impotence, the therapist believes this is a physical manifestation of Chris's more psychological and emotional disturbance. From the start of the story it is apparent that Chris's armour is still very much in place. He is the only client to venture forth in the treacherous snow that morning. Other clients have requested telephone or video call sessions.

- What arrangements might you make with your clients when reaching your consulting room is extremely difficult; for example, when there is, as in the story, deep snow or floods, or a railway closure or tube strike?
- Do you agree to have telephone or video call sessions? How would you justify this or what might be your objections to making such arrangements?
- If you take a view that does not permit these alternatives, would you charge your client for the missed session? Under what circumstances might you not charge? What is your rationale for either of these positions?
- What is your general policy concerning missed sessions and payment? How did you come to this decision and what are the pros and cons of your policy?

In relation to Chris and his presenting problem of impotence:

- Do you agree with the therapist's view that Chris's impotence is likely to be a symptom of his psychological and emotional disturbance? (pp. 95–96) If not, what is your view? How would your approach differ?
- Persistent erectile dysfunction often has a physical cause such as high blood pressure, drug and alcohol abuse, the side effects of medication, diabetes, Parkinson's disease, and others. As Chris attends his GP appointments, we may assume from the story that the therapist is satisfied these physical

possibilities have been checked out. Would you refer your client to their GP in similar circumstances? Why or why not? What other physical complaints might lead you to suggest a medical consultation?

- The therapist does not directly address Chris's impotence at all, nor does he explore his sex life with Maria. How would you address the issue of impotence with your client? Would you give at least some attention to the sex life of your client with his partner? What would be your rationale for doing so or not?

When Chris generalises about people and is critical of their weakness (p. 91), the therapist brings himself into the equation saying "that must include me" (p. 91).

- Why do you think he does this? What is he trying to achieve?
- Do you consider this to be useful or not?
- Is this how you might work? Why or why not?
- What is the therapeutic value and what are the pitfalls of such an approach?

Their exchange has relevance later in the story, but at this time the therapist allows the focus to move away from their relationship to Maria as he ponders his avoidance of intimacy with Chris (pp. 92–93).

- Do you feel critical of the therapist for allowing this? How might you have handled this exchange?
- Can you think of times when you have allowed the focus to shift away from the relationship between you and your client? What were you feeling and thinking at the time?
- How do you manage your own feelings of discomfort when working relationally in this way with your clients?

After one session, the therapist goes down to help Chris with his snowshoes (p. 95), which has positive and therapeutic repercussions later in the work (pp. 96–97). The therapist is of the opinion that "sometimes … it's the after session—the off-guard moments between therapist and client—that has a more profound effect than what transpires in the prescribed fifty minutes" (p. 95). It seems his old supervisor might have objected to what he did.

- Do you agree with the therapist's opinion? Why or why not?
- Would you have helped Chris with his snowshoes? Why or why not?
- What examples do you have of such after session, off-guard moments being therapeutically important, if not profound, from your own practice?
- Have there been any such moments in your own personal therapy? What gave them their importance to you specifically?
- What are your limits to such extracurricular interventions? Where do you draw the line and what reasons do you have for your boundary?
- Do you agree with the supervisor's opinion that "Gratification is an avoidance of grieving" or with the therapist's belief that sometimes both "the deficit and the grief may surface by being met" (pp. 96–97)? On what do you base your opinion? What examples from your own practice do you have that support your view?

The therapist hypothesises how Chris's childhood experiences—the modelling, verbal admonishments, physical neglect and violent abuse—had "necessitated the growth of his armadillo's armour" (p. 97).

- Do you agree with his hypothesis? Do you consider that such childhood experiences would inevitably influence anyone and everyone to become armoured like Chris? If not,

179

how would you account for differences of outcome? What other factors do you take into account?

- How does your model or approach help to explain the development of a personality with such characteristics as Chris's?
- What are the aspects of your chosen theories that provide an understanding of the effects of childhood experiences on adult personality?

Chris's expression of his feelings seems cathartic but is not enough to fully resolve his problem of impotence. The therapist suggests that "insight, a precursor to choice, is invaluable in creating a more holistic connection, especially for someone like Chris" (pp. 97–98).

- What do you think he is saying here? Do you agree?
- Would you say that your approach emphasises emotional expression over insight (or vice versa) or is it a balance of the two? Or might this vary from client to client—in which case, on what considerations do you base your emphasis?
- Chris appears to gain his own insight into the dynamic interface between the past and the present in relation to intimacy (pp. 100–101), but what is the therapist's role here? Do you find him too directive, suggestive, or leading? If you were his supervisor, how might you critique his interventions in this part of the story?

In case you didn't get it, the answer to the crossword clue *"Musical postulant, confused with toy mannequin, unearths New World Digger (9 letters)"* on page 102 is the nine-letter word that is the title of the story: Armadillo. The postulant or pre-novice nun is Maria from the musical *The Sound of Music*. The toy mannequin is a Doll. If you confuse or mix up these letters, you unearth or discover a New World (American) digger (an animal that digs), which is, of course, an ARMADILLO.

Seven deadly sins

Long before the end of the story you may have rightly guessed that this romp through the therapist's day is not real but a terrible nightmare peopled by several clients who, along with the therapist's own behaviours, represent each of the seven deadly sins. However, before examining them in turn, I wonder what your experience is of having dreams about your clients.

- How do you feel when a client has entered your dream world?
- How often does this happen and how many of your clients have you had dreams about?
- What roles do your clients take in your dreams?
- What significance do you give these "appearances"?
- Do you find they help or hinder your work with clients? In what way?
- Do you share your dreams with your clients? Why or why not?
- Do you take your dreams of clients to supervision? Why or why not?
- If yes to either of the above, what have been your clients' or supervisor's responses?
- The therapist's dream leaves him disturbed but he hopes to "bracket off this sense of unease well enough to work with my clients" (p. 103). Whether it's a dream or some other experience, how do you manage any disturbing feelings you may have prior to seeing a client?

Lolita, representing LUST, is a challenge in many ways, not only in her belief that she is forty years younger than the therapist thinks she is (p. 104) but in her bold and salacious behaviour towards him (p. 105). One might well question the therapist's unconscious in having such an extremely sexualised older woman appearing in his dream, and I could hazard some guesses—but as I know as little as you about Michael Martin's erotic, unconscious processes, I think it best left there. But what about you?

- Have you had erotic dreams involving your clients?
- How have you felt about having such dreams?
- Have they enhanced or inhibited your work with those clients?
- Do you take these dreams to supervision? Was this helpful? How?
- Might there be occasions when you would share your erotic dreams (or even waking fantasies) with the client concerned. Why or why not? What are the important questions to ask yourself in this situation? What are the likely repercussions? What are the ethical dilemmas around such disclosure?
- Faced with an extremely flirtatious client like Lolita, how would you work with her and her behaviour?
- Do you see the erotic as a normal aspect of the therapeutic relationship? How does your approach to counselling or psychotherapy address erotic dynamics?

For anyone interested in further exploring the place of the erotic in psychotherapy, I would recommend David Mann's *Psychotherapy—An Erotic Relationship* (1997), also his edited *Erotic Transference and Countertransference* (1999), and Maria Luca's edited *Sexual Attraction in Therapy* (2014).

The therapist thinks of other therapists to whom he might refer Lolita but feels guilty "at the thought of foisting the deranged Lolita onto any of them" (p. 105). Given, at some time or another, we all have potential clients with whom we may decide not to work …

- What reasons might you have for making a decision not to work with a particular client?

- How might you address this with the person who hoped to be a potential client? What might be the difficulties, and how might you deal with these difficulties?
- If you had a client like Lolita, how would you feel about referring her on to a colleague?
- Have you had situations where, like Michael Martin, you found it difficult to refer an extremely troubled client? How did you resolve this?

Sloan, representing SLOTH, seems to have attended only a quarter of his sessions and then been late for those (p. 106).

- When a client attends therapy sessions infrequently, how do you address this?
- If a client is late, and if it is possible, do you extend their session to allow the full time? Why or why not? How might this be problematic? How might it be appropriate and useful?
- Do you charge for missed sessions? If so, how do you justify this? If not, why not?
- How might you have responded, if at all, to Sloan's text message (p. 106)?

Greg, in his accumulation of possessions and lovers (representing the sin of GREED) seems to induce ENVY in the therapist, even though he protests that "I'm not envious of the possessions. I'd just like to experience what it's like not to have to think about the utility bills" (p. 108). Whether it's wealth, relationships, professional success, creative talent, athletic prowess, or gymnastic sexual performance, our clients may have achieved success in areas in which we have not.

- How do you manage your own feelings of envy or jealousy when a client presents their achievements and successes?
- Would you ever share such feelings with your client? Why or why not?

- How might you work with someone like Greg for whom the accumulation of possessions is never enough (pp. 107–108)?
- If a client's frame of reference about success (for example, the accumulation of wealth) is far removed from your own, would you address this? How and why?
- Might you find it difficult to be empathic with a client who does not have to think about the utility bills and yet brings issues of scarcity of wealth to the sessions? How might you manage this for yourself and with your client?
- Conversely, if a client expresses envy of what they perceive as your successes or achievements (or comparative affluence), how would you address this?

GLUTTONY is represented by the therapist's raiding of the fridge in his "urgent need to eat" (p. 108). Despite this disturbing dream experience, in his waking life, as far as I know, Michael Martin does not have an eating disorder. He is a little stout but it appears from some of the stories that he is aware of this and attends to his diet accordingly. However, it is likely that he, like most therapists, will have clients who present with eating problems (anorexia nervosa, bulimia, binge eating, and, according to current trends, obesity) at some time or other.

- Do you attend to your own weight and fitness? How do you see this in relation to working as a psychotherapist with clients?
- Would you address your client's obesity even if she or he was not aware of this as a problem? Why or why not?
- Do you feel competent to work with clients who present with eating disorders? If not, what support might you need in order to do so? Or would you refer clients with eating problems? To whom or to where?
- What has been your experience so far in working with such clients? What have been the key issues in your work

together? Has eating been the focus? If not, what has been your approach and was it effective?

For interested readers I would refer to Marilyn Duker and Roger Slade's *Anorexia Nervose and Bulimia: How to Help* (2003) and Giorgio Nardone, Roberta Milanese, and Tiziana Verbitz's *Prison of Food* (2005).

PRIDE is represented by Priddy, whose psychological survival, the therapist suggests, "depends upon others with whom she can compare herself, compete, and proudly emerge as the better of the two" (p. 110). He also says "she defines herself by her desire to be more important, special and attractive than anyone else in her environs" (p. 111).

- In your theoretical approach, how might you describe such a person?
- Apart from the above quotes, what are for you the key elements in the story that would lead to such a description or diagnosis?
- How do you understand the emotional and psychological origins of such a way of being in the world? What style of parenting and what early experiences might lead to a child developing this characterological adaptation?
- In your therapeutic approach, is there a particular style or stance you would adopt when working with someone like Priddy? If so, what might that be? What might you encourage, avoid, manage or respond to particularly in order to help such a client?
- In the story, the therapist believes it is his role "to challenge her fixed perception of the world and her place in it" (p. 111). Do you agree? Why or why not? How might you approach her frame of reference differently?
- Later, the therapist confronts Priddy's grandiosity "in an attempt to force a reality check" (p. 112). Do you think this is helpful or harmful with someone whose psychological

survival seems to depend on seeing themselves in this way? How else might you approach a client's grandiose perceptions of themselves?

For understanding and working with people one might describe as narcissistic, I recommend Stephen Johnson's *Humanizing the Narcissistic Style* (1991), Heinz Kohut's *The Analysis of the Self* (1971) and James Masterson and Anne Lieberman's edited *A Therapist's Guide to the Personality Disorders* (2004).

Ray, the last client in this story, represents WRATH. He appears to be angry towards everyone and everything (including the therapist and even "birds with their flappy wings", p. 114). By turns, the therapist appears to be defensive, scared or confronting in his attempts to deal with Ray's onslaught.

- Understanding, supporting, maybe even encouraging clients in their anger towards people and events both past and present is one thing, but what has been your experience of clients being angry towards you?
- How have you responded to your clients' anger?
- What factors have been influential in how you may have responded differently to different clients being angry with you?
- What differentiates a useful expression of anger towards you from one which feels potentially destructive?
- Have you ever been angry in response? How was this useful or not so useful? How did you work through this rupture together? How did this effect your therapeutic relationship?
- What do you see as the positives in supporting clients to express their anger?

Let's face it

This story opens with the therapist justifying his practice of not charging potential clients for an initial interview (pp. 117–118).

Reflections

- Do you agree with his argument for not charging? If not, how do justify charging for an initial interview?
- How do you view the purpose of an initial interview? What would you hope to explore with your potential client?
- What factors would support your decision whether or not to work with a particular person?
- What do you think the therapist means when he talks of mutuality as "fellow travellers" yet refers to the "asymmetric relationship of therapist and client" (p. 118)?
- Charles does not seem interested in the therapist's qualifications but is satisfied just knowing that he is registered and accredited (p. 118). Is it important to you that your clients know of your qualifications or accreditations? Do you include them in your emails, on letter headings, or websites? Why or why not?

After speaking together on the phone, the therapist reflects on Charles and imagines various aspects of him and his life in some detail (p. 119).

- How might this form of projective imagining help or hinder the initial interview?
- Given that we all create images of people we have not met, have there been times when your projections have been very accurate, or conversely, wildly off track? How do you account for this?

The therapist is accurate in some of his imaginings, but understandably he had not imagined Charles' disfigured face and hand, and he finds this difficult to deal with at first (pp. 119–120).

- How would you deal with the obvious physical injuries, ailments, disabilities or disfigurements of a client on first meeting?

- How do you feel about the way the therapist dealt with Charles' obvious disfigurement?
- Should he have waited until Charles (for whom ostensibly this is not the issue that has brought him to therapy) mentioned it?

Equally, in relation to Charles' discomfort about being gay (which seems to worry him more than his disfigurement), the therapist seems to have difficulty empathising with Charles' concern (p. 122).

- How did you respond when reading of the therapist's apparent lack of understanding?
- How did you feel when the therapist says, "I'm not understanding what it is that is disturbing you so much" (p. 124)? It may be honest, but what are the problems in such a statement? What might the client feel in response?
- How would you respond to a client who was expressing discomfort about her or his sexuality, gender, ethnicity, relationship status, etc.?
- How could the therapist have responded differently?

Eventually, Charles discloses that the impediment to his declaring his attraction to Chris is his belief about his face. He wasn't ready earlier to admit this, explaining, "It needed a context" (p. 125).

- The therapist has his ideas of what Charles meant by this. What are yours?
- In your approach to therapy, what might be another way of describing this "context" within the therapeutic relationship?
- Regarding Charles' story, do you find the therapist's hypothesis about his keeping others at a distance plausible? How else might you understand such behaviour? How might

you describe his way of being in terms of attachment theory (see Bowlby (1969, 1973, 1980))?

- Charles describes the therapist's hypothesis as "psychobabble" (p. 126). How might you respond to such criticism?
- When the therapist realises he has trapped Charles in a double bind (agree with me and I'm correct, protest too much and I'm still correct) he wonders how to extricate Charles from it (p. 127) but, in the event, does not have to. How might he have done this if Charles had not found a grain of truth in it himself?
- At the end of the story, why do you think the therapist believes that not declaring whether he wants to work with Charles or not is "the very heart of his issue" (p. 128)?

Tales out of school

Responding to a letter from a mature student who is undertaking a psychotherapy training, the therapist, Michael Martin, takes the opportunity to have a rant about some aspects of contemporary psychotherapy theory and practice. He may come across as a pompous, grumpy old man (though he would prefer "older") but it might be worth discussing and reflecting on some of what he says.

- You may not agree with his suggesting that theoretical therapy books and articles appear "at an alarming rate" (p. 130) but how do you select what you read from the vast array on offer to support you in your professional development? Do you read solely within your chosen approach? Do you organise your reading around themes or do you read more randomly according to what appeals to you?
- What was the last book or article you read that affected the way you work? Why did it influence you? What was new or different about the author's perspective?

Reflections

- Like Michael, do you find some of the language off-putting? Does the language influence your choice of what to read?
- How does your approach to therapy address unconscious processes and how do you work with such processes in your therapy with clients?
- The language may be different, but does your approach include concepts such as intersubjectivity (p. 131), transference, countertransference, projection, introjection, splitting, unformulated experience, and co-creation (p. 133) or enactment and mutual relational influence (p. 135)? How would you explain each of these to a non-therapist?
- How do you view and work with "Freudian slips" such as the one Michael's client may have made in addressing him as Ian? Do you agree with Michael that sometimes "a cigar is just a cigar" (p. 135)?
- How do you respond to the therapist's view of what he calls "bogus intersubjectivity" (p. 136)? Have you experienced yourself disclosing something that was therapist-centred rather than client-centred, or have you, as a client, felt overlooked in favour of the therapist taking centre stage? How have you addressed either of these situations and what was the outcome?
- In working with someone like Bob (pp. 138–140), who believes that everyone, including you, his therapist, hates him, how might you address his generalised negativity? Can you imagine yourself saying to such a client that you are not his mother? How might you justify such an intervention?
- Do you share this therapist's understanding of rupture and repair (pp. 140–143)? If not, what is your understanding? Do you believe it is necessary to disturb your clients, if not at every session, regularly (p. 142) in order to be "doing psychotherapy"? Why or why not? What might be the grain of truth in such an idea?
- What do you think the therapist means when he talks of the child "reconfiguring her internal world" (p. 141)?

• Do you read much fiction? Do you agree with the therapist that reading fiction enhances your understanding and practice as a psychotherapist? Why or why not?

For those readers interested in some of the concepts raised in this final story, I would refer you to, regarding intersubjectivity and unconscious processes: *Affect Regulation, Mentalization, and the Development of the Self* (2002) by Peter Fonagy et al.; Stephen Mitchell's *Relationality: From Attachment to Intersubjectivity* (2000); Donnel Stern's *Partners in Thought* (2010); and Robert Stolorow, George Atwood, and Bernard Brandchaft's *The Intersubjective Perspective* (1994). Regarding rupture and repair: Michael Kahn's *Between Therapist and Client: The New Relationship* (1991); Heinz Kohut's *How Does Analysis Cure?* (1984); Jeremy Safran and Christopher Muran's *Negotiating the Therapeutic Alliance* (2000); and Carole Shadbolt's *The Place of Failure in Rupture and Repair* (2012).

References

Bender, M., Bauckham, P., & Norris, A. (1999). *The Therapeutic Purpose of Reminiscence*. London: Sage.

Berne, E. (1964). *Games People Play*. New York: Grove Press.

Berne, E. (1972). *What Do You Say After You Say Hello?* New York: Grove Press.

Bowlby, J. (1969). *Attachment and Loss (Vol. 1: Attachment.)* New York: Basic.

Bowlby, J. (1973). *Attachment and Loss (Vol. 2: Separation: Anxiety and Anger)*. New York: Basic.

Bowlby, J. (1980). *Attachment and Loss (Vol. 3: Loss: Sadness and Depression)*. New York: Basic.

Carroll, M. (2014). *Effective Supervision for the Helping Professions* (2nd edn). London: Sage.

Carroll, M., & Gilbert, M. C. (2011). *On Being a Supervisee: Creating Learning Partnerships*. Ealing: Vukani Publishing.

Claringbull, N. (2010). *What is Counselling and Psychotherapy?* Exeter: Learning Matters.

Clarkson, P. (1995). *The Therapeutic Relationship in Psychoanalysis, Counselling and Psychotherapy*. London: Whurr.

Cohn, H. W. (1997). *Existential Thought and Therapeutic Practice*. London: Sage.

Cooper, M. (2003). *Existential Therapies*. London: Sage.

Cooper, M. (2008). *Essential Research Findings in Counselling and Psychotherapy—The Facts Are Friendly*. London: Sage.

References

Davies, D., & Neal, C. (2000). *Therapeutic Perspectives on Working with Lesbian, Gay and Bisexual Clients*. Buckingham: Open University Press.

DeYoung, P. A. (2003). *Relational Psychotherapy: A Primer*. New York: Brunner-Routledge.

DSM-5 (2013). *DSM-5 Diagnostic and Statistical Manual of Mental Disorders* (5th edn). Washington, DC: American Psychiatric Association.

Duker, M., & Slade, R. (2003). *Anorexia Nervosa and Bulimia: How to Help* (2nd edn). Buckingham: Open University Press.

Etherington, K. (Ed.) (2003). *Trauma, the Body and Transformation: A Narrative Inquiry*. London: Jessica Kingsley.

Fairbairn, W. R. D. (1952). *Psychoanalytic Studies of the Personality*. London: Tavistock.

Fonagy, P., Gergely, G., Jurist, E. L., & Target, M. (2002). *Affect Regulation, Mentalization, and the Development of the Self*. New York: Other Press.

Gelso, C. J., & Carter, J. A. (1985). The Relationship in counselling and psychotherapy: Components, consequences and theoretical antecedents. *Counselling Psychologist, 13*(2): 155–243.

Gibson, F. (2011). *Reminiscence and Life Story Work: A Practical Guide*. London: Jessica Kingsley.

Gilbert, M. C., & Evans, K. (2000). *Psychotherapy Supervision: An Integrative, Relational Approach to Psychotherapy Supervision*. Buckingham: Open University Press.

Gilbert, M. C., & Shmukler, D. (1996). *Brief Therapy with Couples*. West Sussex: John Wiley & Sons.

Golden, M. (2005). *Don't Play in the Sun: One Woman's Journey Through the Color Complex*. New York: Anchor.

Greenberg, E. (1989). Healing the Borderline. *The Gestalt Journal* Vol 12 (2) pp. 11–15.

Hawkins, P., & Shohet, R. (2012). *Supervision in the Helping Professions* (4th edn). Berkshire: Open University Press.

Heidegger, M. (1962). *Being and Time* (Trans. Macquarrie J., & Robinson, E.). Oxford: Blackwell, 1926.

ICD-10 (1992). *The ICD-10 Classification of Mental and Behavioural Disorders*. Geneva: World Health Organisation.

References

Johnson, S. (1987). *Humanizing the Narcissistic Style*. New York: Norton.

Johnson, S. (1994). *Character Styles*. New York: Norton.

Joines, V., & Stewart, I. (2002). *Personality Adaptations*. Nottingham and Chapel Hill, NC: Lifespace Publishing.

Kahn, M. (1991). *Between Therapist and Client: The New Relationship*. New York: Henry Holt.

Kernberg, O. (1975). *Borderline Conditions and Pathological Narcissism*. Northvale, NJ: J. Aronson.

Kernberg, O. (1984). *Severe Personality Disorders*. New Haven, CT: Yale University Press.

Kohut, H. (1971). *The Analysis of the Self: A Systematic Approach to the Psychoanalytic Treatment of Narcissistic Personality Disorders*. New York: International Universities Press.

Kohut, H. (1984). *How Does Analysis Cure?* Chicago: University of Chicago Press.

Kreisman, J. J., & Straus, H. (1989). *I Hate You—Don't Leave Me: Understanding the Borderline Personality*. New York: Avon.

Kubler-Ross, E. (1970). *On Death and Dying*. London: Tavistock.

Lago, C., & Smith, B. (Eds.) (2010). *Anti-Discriminatory Practice in Counselling and Psychotherapy* (2nd edn). London: Sage.

Lapworth, P., & Sills, C. (2011). *An Introduction to Transactional Analysis*. London: Sage.

Litvinoff, S. (2001). *The Relate Guide to Better Relationships: Practical Ways to Make Your Love Last*. London: Vermilion.

Lowe, F. (Ed.) (2014). *Thinking Space: Promoting Thinking About Race, Culture, and Diversity in Psychotherapy and Beyond*. London: Karnac.

Luca, M. (2014). *Sexual Attraction in Therapy: Clinical Perspectives on Moving Beyond the Taboo: A Guide for Training and Practice*. West Sussex: John Wiley & Sons.

Mann, D. (1997). *Psychotherapy—An Erotic Relationship: Transference and Countertransference Passions*. London: Routledge.

Mann, D. (1999). *Erotic Transference and Countertransference: Clinical Practice in Psychotherapy*. London: Routledge.

Mann, D., & Cunningham, V. (Eds.) (2009). *The Past in the Present*. East Sussex: Routledge.

References

Maroda, K. J. (2004). *The Power of the Countertransference: Innovations in Analytic technique*. Hillsdale, NJ: The Analytic Press.

Masterson, J. F. (1988). *The Search for the Real Self: Unmasking the Personality Disorders of Our Age*. New York: Macmillan.

Masterson, J. F., & Lieberman, A. R. (Eds.) (2004). *A Therapist's Guide to the Personality Disorders*. Phoenix, AZ: Zeig, Tucker & Theisen.

McLoughlin, B. (1995). *Developing Psychodynamic Counselling*. London: Sage.

McMahon, G., Palmer, S., & Wilding, C. (2005). *The Essential Skills for Setting Up a Counselling and Psychotherapy Practice*. East Sussex: Routledge.

Menninger, K. (1958). *The Theory of Psychoanalytic Technique*. New York: Basic.

Mitchell, S. A. (2000). *Relationality: From Attachment to Intersubjectivity*. Hillsdale, NJ: The Analytic Press.

Nardone, G., Milanese, R., & Verbitz, T. (2005). *Prison of Food: Research and Treatment of Eating Disorders*. London: Karnac.

Neal, C., & Davies, D. (2000). *Issues in Therapy With Lesbian, Gay, Bisexual and Transgender Clients*. Buckingham: Open University Press.

Rothschild, B. (2000). *The Body Remembers: The Psychophysiology of Trauma and Trauma Treatment*. New York: Norton.

Ryde, J. (2009). *Being White in the Helping Professions*. London: Jessica Kingsley.

Safran, J. D., & Muran, J. C. (2000). *Negotiating the Therapeutic Alliance: A Relational Treatment Guide*. New York: Guilford Press.

Sanderson, C. (2006). *Counselling Adult Survivors of Child Sexual Abuse*. London: Jessica Kingsley.

Shadbolt, C. (2004). Homophobia and gay affirmative transactional analysis. *Transactional Analysis Journal, 34*(2): 113–125.

Shadbolt, C. (2012). The place of failure in rupture and repair. *Transactional Analysis Journal, 42*(1): 5–16.

Spinelli, E. (1989). *The Interpreted World: An Introduction to Phenomenological Psychology*. London: Sage.

Stark, M. (1999). *Modes of Therapeutic Action*. Northvale, NJ: Jason Aronson.

References

Stern, B. B. (2010). *Partners in Thought: Working with Unformulated Experience, Dissociation, and Enactment.* East Sussex: Routledge.

Stewart, I., & Joines, V. (1987). *TA Today: A New Introduction to Transactional Analysis.* London: Sage.

Stolorow, R. D., Atwood, G. E., & Brandchaft, B. (1994). *The Intersubjective Perspective.* Northvale, NJ: Jason Aronson.

Straker, G. (2006). Signing with a scar: Understanding self-harm. *Psychoanalytic Dialogues, 16*(1): 93–112.

Thompson, N. (2002). *Loss and Grief.* Basingstoke: Palgrave.

Van der Kolk, B. (2014). *The Body Keeps the Score: Mind, Brain and Body in the Transformation of Trauma.* London: Allen Lane.

Van Deurzen, E. (1988). *Existential Counselling in Practice.* London: Sage.

Wachtel, P. L. (2008). *Relational Theory and the Practice of Psychotherapy.* New York: Guilford.

Ware, P. (1983). Personality adaptations. *Transactional Analysis Journal, 13*(1): 11–19.

Wheeler, S. (Ed.) (2006). *Difference and Diversity in Counselling: Contemporary Psychodynamic Perspectives.* New York: Palgrave Macmillan.

Acknowledgements

My grateful thanks to: Laurie, Leo & Kerrie Lapworth for their constant loving support; Laurie for his wonderful cover image; Leo for his photogenic ear; Olivia Lousada for her encouragement of my writing over many years; Charlotte Sills for her faith in my writing and for giving invaluable feedback; Rod Tweedy and the staff at Karnac for their kind interest and generous support of this project; and, finally, my clients and supervisees for sharing with me their real stories and teaching me so much.

About the author

Phil Lapworth is a psychotherapist and supervisor in private practice near Bath. He has been an external examiner, consultant, and supervisor for several integrative counselling and psychotherapy courses and was Director of Clinical Services at the Metanoia Institute in London before moving to Bath.

His interest in psychology and psychotherapy began while a teacher in Special Education, particularly through his work at the Maudsley Psychiatric Hospital School. His subsequent deputy headship at a school for troubled children and adolescents provided him with the opportunity in 1981 to undertake a counselling training at South West London College that encompassed several approaches to counselling.

From these eclectic beginnings, Phil qualified as a transactional analyst, trained in gestalt and, later, integrative psychotherapy, and established a psychotherapy and supervision practice working with adults some thirty years ago. With Charlotte Sills and Sue Fish, he published books on transactional analysis and gestalt approaches and, individually, several chapters and articles in psychotherapy publications.

Through his clinical experience, personal therapy, and further MSc studies, Phil's perspective widened in the nineties, and gave rise to another book with Charlotte and Sue on psychotherapy integration. A second edition of *Integration in Counselling and Psychotherapy: Developing a Personal Approach* was published by Sage in 2010 and, due to their popularity, their earlier introductory books on Transactional Analysis and Gestalt (rewritten and updated to include coaching and other applications, Billy Desmond joining them on the Gestalt book) were published by Sage in 2011 and 2012 respectively.

Encouraged by the inclusion of one of his stories in *Tales of Psychotherapy* (Karnac, 2007), his first foray into fictional short stories about therapy, he went on to publish a collection of stories in *Tales from the Therapy Room: Shrink-Wrapped* (Sage, 2011). This and his current collection, *Listen Carefully* (Karnac, 2014), reflect not only Phil's enjoyment of writing fiction but his continuing interest in, and encouragement of, an integrative, relational, and personal approach to psychotherapy.